CRYSTAL SYMONE

From Seoul With Love Part Two

City of Lights

Contents

Acknowledgments

I want to thank God for the gift that keeps on giving to write another work of fiction. It's easy to have an idea, but with faith and consistency to truly see it through comes new possibilities and stories.

Thank you to the readers for your feedback, truth, and honesty. Indie Authors are not always the first or second choice, but it's nice to know there are still people out there who support us.

Lastly, thanks to family and friends who have supported this dream of mine over the years. Your love is appreciated and valued.

I

Part One

Chapter 1: Welcome Back

"What do you mean; I wasn't supposed to find out?"

These are the words I remember uttering to the man I'd spent the last few months getting to know. Jun Pyo had started to chip away at the walls I'd held up for so long. The walls in my heart that barely came down for anyone ever since I got an abortion at seventeen in secret, one I was forced into by my mother.

But in Seoul, I was trying to break old habits. Yet, based on the postcard in my hands, I can see I keep choosing the same man. Or maybe it's not them; it's me, the one who gives it up so easily and still expects that true love, or whatever fantasy I've been clinging to, is supposed to happen. That it will happen.

The flight from Seoul back to the States feels like an eternity, much like the first time I flew for over twenty-four hours. This time around, my mind is plagued with thoughts of how everything went so wrong. After listening to Jun Pyo repeat, "you weren't supposed to find out like this," I woke up from my stupor and eventually realized that even though being in his arms, his presence, being face-to-face with him seemed like the safest place for me to be, it was quite the opposite.

All he could do was keep saying he was sorry, but sorry didn't explain why he lied to me. Sorry was not going to give me my life back, and sorry sure as hell wouldn't heal my heart or rebuild the trust that had crumbled away when it came to any man in a romantic sense.

After being fired or, as the Force likes to call it, reassigned per the call I received just thirty minutes after my meeting, I learned that my reassignment included a demotion, a pay decrease, and a new stationary assignment in the middle of nowhere, Idaho, until further notice. In addition to that, I'd been issued a letter of reprimand, which is equivalent to being written up for disciplinary action.

My dreams of working my way up the internal ladder and one day becoming one of the few Black women Chief Master Sergeants were gone. I'd be lucky to just get reassigned somewhere else with this kind of record. I thought about quitting or going AWOL right then and there, but I remembered all the hell that comes with that type of move. Right now, I just need to focus on getting out of Seoul.

Any pride I had left for myself disappeared into the evening once I made it back to my apartment. I checked my phone and saw countless texts and calls, some from Dak, asking how the plan worked out. But most of them were from Jun Pyo, pleading with me to understand that he had no choice but to toy with me the way he did. Yet even with "no choice," there was still no explanation, not even a solid reason he could give me for playing these sick mind games.

I took the train back to my military housing and didn't even try to hide from the strangers I passed on the streets. I was sure my face looked a mess, with smeared makeup and eyes red from crying. But not even the strange glances caught much of my attention. All I could think about was making it back to my place. At least there, I could feel some comfort, some safety, and possibly a little peace.

A pain in my feet reminded me that walking long distances in heels is a recipe for disaster. I trudged up to the fifth floor, barely aware that once I reached the doorway and searched for my keys, someone was already standing there waiting for me. Jun Pyo.

I thought my eyes were deceiving me, but the closer I got, the more I knew this was no trick. My eyes weren't playing games with me.

"So you make me look stupid, cause me to lose my job, and now stalk me all in the same day?" I scream, not caring if my neighbors hear.

"Maverick, please let's go inside and talk about this. I promise I can explain everything; you just have to trust me."

"Have to? I did trust you. I was starting to trust you even more than you know. But look where that's gotten me. I don't really know who you even are, and I'm done trying to find out. Now move away from my door and away from me," I say harshly, not holding back. I push past him just as a fresh set of tears starts spilling onto my face. He moves aside quickly but seems reluctant to give up.

I unlock the door and take another look at him standing there, looking so stupid in black slacks and a white button-up shirt, the first two buttons undone, and I can see the top of his chest hair. The shirt is thin enough for me to see his muscles flex underneath, but then I look back at his face.

"Do you really want to know what happened to Violetta Stone?"

My grimace turns less angry at the mention of her name, my body in the doorway, and him outside. I debate whether I should even consider letting him back into my place.

"Yes, I want to know."

"Okay, I will tell you, just please let me in."

Not saying another word, I move my body sideways at the door, allowing him to walk in. For the umpteenth time today, my heart has acted in disobedience to my mind. Against my better judgment, he's crossed the threshold.

Not bothering to hide any emotion, I push him for more, sticking to the point.

"What do you have to tell me about Violetta? Because other than that and the full truth about who you are, I'm not interested in anything else you have to say."

Before speaking, Jun Pyo takes multiple shallow breaths, his chest noticeably rising. He looks at me and then at the door, second-guessing himself and what he's about to share. My patience thins, just seething as I look at him.

"Tell me now, or leave and never come back."

"Okay. I'm sorry. It's just once I say this, nothing can be taken back."

"It's too late for that... again. Tell me now, or leave. I have no time for any more games."

"This is the truth... I mean, everything you found out was true," he stutters.

My mouth falls open, and no words escape. I just clasp my hands over my lips, waiting to hear more.

"My sister and I, when we left North Korea as kids, had nowhere to go. There weren't many places children of an assumed treasonous father could go. We needed help. My sister tried her best, but without an eomma and appa, we were lost souls on the streets once we arrived in South Korea. The only people willing to take us in were gangsters, criminals, and bad people. They made us think they cared about us, but really, they were preparing us to be just like them, to be loyal. So loyal that you'd turn against the only blood relative you know."

"The Crimson Lotus Syndicate isn't just who I work for, I mean, used to work for, they were my family. Suni and I didn't know our lives would become their lives. You don't just sever a connection with the Lotus and live to tell the story."

Still impatient and needing more, I interrupt him.

"How is Violetta mixed up in this?"

"She... she was just collateral. The Lotus had people they wanted me to give them access to, and Violetta was getting too close to finding out the truth. So they put her in a position where no one would believe her. It was impossible. I tried everything to keep them from framing her, but it couldn't be avoided. They wanted to murder her, but I pleaded with them to let her live, saying prison would be better than death if they could make it look like she'd been doing the work instead of me. I knew it wasn't right, but it was the only way I could protect myself and my sister. She's all I've got left."

My heart stings. She's all he has left.

"And what about me? Why did they try to make me fall in love with I mean, why did they want you to sleep with me?"

He grimaces at my blunt words but continues.

"They wanted me to get close to you, but would never say why. I was supposed to make sure we were together in case you started looking at things you shouldn't have, so I could alert the Lotus if you became suspicious of what I was really doing. At first, I told them you were curious about Violetta but didn't have any evidence. Then, when you started researching my file and the Lotus, they began asking more questions. They wanted me to do more things... things I wasn't comfortable with."

"Oh, you mean like sleeping with me?" I say, my frustration peaking again as I think about the text I read.

"Yes. They wanted me to do that and other things... tracking you, even poisoning you once you revealed the truth. They are good at making people disappear and even better at hiding evidence that implicates their organization. I did what I could to protect you, but now that I've compromised my own safety, I can't stay in this city, let alone the country. And that's the truth. But what I started to feel for you made me want to disobey their orders."

His eyes steady on me, and I look away quickly, not wanting to get caught up in his rapture.

* * *

I don't know how we ended up here again, but somehow, he's become the most intoxicating thing to me. I lay on my bed with my back pressed into the mattress while he's lying on top of me. SORRY. It seems that's the only proper word he can utter. My pulse quickens again as he kisses my tears away from my cheek. There is barely any space between us as he explains that he's going to show me just how sorry he is, claiming he'll make up for his betrayal. The way he whispers in my ear and speaks Korean when he can't explain what he wants in English is driving me mad. It's like he's pinned me down so I can't run, and even though it should feel like torture, the more he talks, the more it starts to feel like a haven.

So what if he lied?

Even though the answers to these questions inside me go unanswered, I can't seem to pull myself away from this man. In such a short time, his hold on me is as strong as a baby's grip. I can't let go yet.

"Maverick, I need you... I want to be with you, but I'm not sure how to be. These people will... kill you and me." He continues whispering, as if someone else were in my apartment. Since he's positioned his body on top of mine, I avoid looking into his eyes, afraid I'll completely cave in. Isn't it stupid that I would rather give in to him than give him what he deserves?

I open my eyes fully and finally give him what he's been asking for: my full attention. Afraid to even speak, worried my voice will betray what I know needs to happen, I just stare at him. He seems shocked that I'm acknowledging him this way and stops whispering. Without warning, he presses his lips to mine. And the feeling it sends through my body is like eating a pint of butter pecan ice cream on a cheat day. My mouth waters with excitement, even though my mind isn't in agreement. I am wrong. He is wrong. But somehow, when our mouths connect, it feels right. He begins to press against my lower thigh, and even though I said I wouldn't speak, a moan slips from my mouth. He takes it as an invitation, tugging gently and intentionally at my skirt and tights while his lips continue to move in rhythm with mine.

I'm not sure if I want to do this, but a part of me feels like this is the last time our last time and maybe I should focus on that because it's easier. Not hard, like everything else will be moving forward.

His hands slide down into my panties, and I can't tell if it's the moment or the knowledge that this will be our last time, but his touch makes me feel painfully sensitive. I close my eyes, unable to keep making eye contact with him. He touches me softly, sweetly. If only this were who he truly was, instead of a man wrapped in secrets who betrayed me. I pant for air as he wipes his damp hands onto the bed sheet.

But just when I think I won't be swayed, I feel him. He's

worked his way inside me, and his apology and regret seem to spill out in the way his body moves with mine. I can feel his muscles tighten against me with every quickened pace. He grips my shoulder so I can't pull away. We are so close, closer than we've ever been, and the tears return as I wonder what kind of woman would allow him back into such a sacred place after all of this.

Me. That's who.

As we both climax quickly, I look into his eyes, wondering who he really is.

"I can't seem to let you go," he says softly.

* * *

Staring down at my nimble hands, I'm back in Charleston, stuck with my mom, in my childhood room, and even worse, with no sense of purpose. My thumbnail rubs against the postcard, the red polish and red stamp seeming to match one another. The imprint of the stamp rises above the smooth surface of the white postcard. I flip it over in my hand. Back and forth. Back and forth. Should I even reread it for the twentieth time?

It was addressed to me, with no return address or even a mention of the sender. But a picture of the Namsan Tower looms on the front of the postcard, and I know now it's him. On the back, in small, delicate cursive, it's exactly as I remember from watching Jun Pyo sign off on our reports. His handwriting used to annoy me because it was so hard to read, but I learned to adjust. Looking at the way each letter curves into the next, I can't help but picture him sitting wherever he is, writing this to me.

Holding the small piece of paper in the air as my head rests on my childhood collection of stuffed elephants and a sky blue pillow, all I can think is not again. I start reading the postcard.

From a friend, I'm sorry I hurt you in the way I did.

He must be referring to how he used me, slept with me, and then ruined my career. Some friend. Hell, I thought we were more than friends.

Everything I shared with you was real, but I had to protect myself and my family. I had no choice in the matter. But know that I will make this right and protect you. Ever since I saw you and I mean really saw you, all I've wanted to do is protect you. When the time is right, meet me at the place where love can never be unlocked in the City of Light.

Next to a small drawn heart are the words From Seoul, With Love.

My life has spiraled faster than I can make sense of. It's only been three months since I stopped doing what I loved, since I lost my independence and my hope of ever trusting a man again in this lifetime. They've hurt me when I wanted to please them. Hurt me when I tried to be fearless in the pursuit of love. It didn't matter whether I was compromising my well-being or my body; they didn't seem to care. Somehow, in the equation that is them and me, I always come last.

And in last place, there isn't much room to feel anything but bitterness.

I throw the letter down on my comforter and stare up at the ceiling, contemplating how everything spun so far out of control that I ended up here.

Chapter 2: The Secret

The aroma of Sunday dinner fills the air with barbecue ribs, mac and cheese, and sweet potato pie. My father's favorites are the wonderful smells filling my parents' two-story brick home. Today is a special day: my father's sixtieth birthday. He's been my hero for as long as I can remember. Through numerous active duty assignments and countless special missions, he inspired me. Although my mother and I were often indifferent toward one another, I always admired the love my father showed her and us. I just wish I could find someone like him for myself.

He was the type of man who never once talked about my mother splitting the bills with him. He believed it was his duty to manage the finances. I can remember him being on active duty, yet he never missed a call or an update on how life was going back home. He showed me what a man should do, but somehow, that example never quite reflected in the men I chose.

Out of his seventy years of life, he and my mother have been married for over forty years, and he never chose infidelity, never had outside children, and never abused my mom. They don't make men like him anymore, I think silently to myself.

I get up from the bed and stare down into the backyard, set up with plastic tables and chairs and green and gray decorations from Party City. The house is still quiet as we wait for our extended family members to arrive. A string of green balloons lines the wooden deck my father built with his bare hands when I was seven. There are tiki torches, a special reserved area for the bartender my mother hired, and a row of metal horseshoes toward the back of the yard. Everything is ready, and as I look down at the tan-and-blue sundress I'm wearing, I smooth it over my legs, wondering what else this celebration might bring.

I'm mostly overjoyed to celebrate my father, but in the back of my mind, I'm also dreading today. There will be many questions my family will ask me why I'm back living with my parents, why I don't have a man or kids, or why I look bigger and not as skinny as they remember me being fifteen years ago. A flood of prepared answers runs through my head, trying to quiet my nerves.

I'm really not in the mood to be questioned, but in my family, nosiness seems to come with the territory. Still, I'll put on a strong face for my dad; he deserves it.

I notice my father step outside briefly to lift the large grill hood and check on the food. He has enough ribs, grilled chicken, and hamburgers to feed a small army. Smoke spills from the grill, drifting up to my nostrils as I inhale through the open window. He flips the meat expertly, rubbing the ribs with his homemade barbecue sauce a recipe he would protect at all costs. Nearby, in a small deep fryer, fish crackles in hot oil. He lifts the basket from the bubbling grease and lets the fillets cool.

His salt and pepper goatee frames his face as he looks up and smiles, dressed in his comfortable attire. He's wearing a wide brimmed sun hat from his fishing trips, a green plaid shirt, and khaki shorts. I wave at him before glancing down at my smartwatch.

Six o'clock. Nearly time for the party to begin.

I exit my room and walk down the stairs, nearly colliding with my mom at the bottom of the staircase near the patio door. She's carrying a stack of sweet potato pies out to the dessert table. We are both stunned for a moment as the pies wobble but don't fall from her hands. There are at least six pies, all homemade, that fill her arms. Temporarily distracted by the smell, I imagine all my cousins, aunts, and uncles pining away over the pies, each one worth every single bit of work my mother put in.

"I'm sorry, I didn't realize you were coming down, Mavvy. Would you mind grabbing the door since you're here?"

"It's fine, I didn't see you either, Mom. Here, I've got the door." I extend the patio door open, allowing my mother to walk by. Following her to the dessert table, I arrange a few napkins and plates. The table is almost full, with a large buttercream sheet cake featuring pictures of my father from different times in his life. In addition, peach cobbler, banana pudding, and a rum cake sit on the table. My mother slides the pies into a small corner, making sure they're secure.

"So, who all is coming to the party today?"

I'm curious about who my mother has invited. Between my mother and father, they have nine siblings and a host of cousins, friends from church, and buddies from their senior group who go on trips and activities together. Admiring the spacious backyard, I notice at least fifty seats set for guests at tables spread out.

"Mostly some people from church, but you know, family will be here. Your Aunt Shirley and all your dad's siblings Bobby, Drew, Wanda, and Jill should all be here."

Thinking of my aunts and uncles brings back memories of

a simpler time. My Aunt Shirley was my mom's sister. They were the closest to one another, but my mom's other siblings were estranged.

There was Samantha, the professional liar, who had been arrested multiple times for petty theft and, the last time I heard, had gotten into credit card fraud. At forty-five, she was the youngest but wildest sibling my mother had. She wasn't allowed around much because my mother felt she was a bad influence. She was probably right.

The second youngest was my Uncle Sherman, but everyone called him Sherm. He had five kids with three different women. He was a ladies' man, and even at the age of fifty, he still couldn't be bothered with the thought of marriage and being tied down. Although his heart was the size of the moon, he always showed love wherever he went. My mother's relationship with Uncle Sherm was close, but not close enough to keep them from butting heads whenever they saw each other.

Aunt Shirley sat in the middle. Growing up, she was the peacekeeper, never took sides, and was always in my mom's corner, from what I remember.

When my grandparents were alive, Aunt Shirley would always take Shaunie and me to visit. My mom never went, but she always made us pass a message along, like, "Tell your grandparents I said hey." Yet, of all the times Aunt Shirley drove the hour-long trip to Edisto, it was always just her, me, and Shaunie.

I never knew why growing up, and to this day, I have never seen my mother acknowledge her relationship with her parents. The only time she's ever shown emotion over them was at their funerals, and even then, that was the extent of her feelings. Something tells me that under that murky water, there's something buried.

Last but not least was my Uncle Charlie, whom my mother couldn't stand the most. He was full of potential and had the opportunity of a lifetime at nineteen to play with The Swirls, an old-school music group that hit big in Hollywood. They were like the Temptations, but bigger. Uncle Charlie was musically gifted, but he ruined his chances with the group because of a drinking problem. Now, in his late sixties, all that's left of him is a weak bladder and a mouth that won't quit. My mother despises him but tolerates him when she has to. He always finds a way to make a situation worse.

"Oh, and your father invited one of your old classmates," she says. "He said he bumped into him at the hardware store. His name was... Jermaine or Jere something. I told him not to just invite anyone to our house, but he said he's a good kid." She continues looking down, pre-cutting a few slices of pie, but she can't hide the snickering smile.

I know darn well who my father bumped into, Jeremiah Simpson. We attended grade school together until the tenth grade. His mother had moved down to Atlanta after getting divorced. We were the best of friends, with naked baby pictures in the tub to cement our bond. We tried to keep up with one another, but grew apart once he moved. It's been ages since we've seen each other, but I know this "invite" is no coincidence.

Feigning little interest, I play along. "Oh, when did he move back?"

"About two months ago. He said he got tired of city life and wanted to be home. He even talked about settling down."

"Mm hmm... and who is trying to set me up?"

"Huh?" my mom says, playing dumb. "I don't know what

you mean. But your father has a mind of his own."

I roll my eyes before walking off. My mom yells over my shoulder, "Can you bring the potato salad out of the fridge, please?"

I keep walking but yell back that I will, though not before rolling my eyes at my parents' obvious attempt to set me up. Opening the patio door, I walk toward the kitchen, but hear the doorbell and head to the front door instead.

Looking through the round glass window, I can see that it's my Aunt Shirley who has arrived first. I smile, waving through the window, then quickly open the screen door to hug her. I hold onto her like a child, feeling the warmth of her round flesh.

"Well, if it isn't my niece Maverick... girl, you are a sight for sore eyes. How are you doing, dear?"

I pull away slightly from our embrace to answer, "Auntie, it hasn't been that long, but I've missed you too. I'm doing well," I say vaguely, but smiling.

My aunt gives me the same "Mm hmm" rebuttal I just gave my mom, but she doesn't pester me for more information. She adds, "We're going to talk later, and I mean really talk."

"But anyway, where's your mother at?"

"She's outside setting up."

"Alright. I had to pick up your Uncle Charlie from his Alcoholics Anonymous meeting, so he's in the car. I told him to give me a few minutes before he came in. You know how your mom and he get."

Yep, I sure do enjoy sharing that with her.

"OK, honey, can't say they'll be any pleasure, but we're family. She'll get over it."

Looking past my aunt, I stare at her beige KIA sedan and see Uncle Charlie opening the door. His tall frame seems thinner, and an army of gray hairs on his balding head and beard makes him look older. His signature gold chain and tooth shine in the light as he smiles at me.

"Niece, is that you? Hey, Shaunie, girl, you've grown."

"Actually, it's Maverick... and yes, I see you have gotten older too," I say, with a snide remark.

"My mistake," he says, throwing his arms up and flailing them. "You know it's been forever since I laid eyes on you."

"Yes, we'll come in," I say awkwardly, not motioning toward him. My aunt stands awkwardly between us.

"You go in. We'll be right behind you."

I open the front door, heading back inside, but not before I hear Aunt Shirley say, "I told you to stay in the car, Charlie. You're just hard-headed."

Shaking my head, I walk back toward the kitchen to grab the potato salad. As I walk back outside, I place the dish on a table for sides and avoid my mother's questioning when she asks what took so long.

I go upstairs, wanting to avoid any drama and long explanations about why Uncle Charlie is here. I enter my room and lean down to reach under my bed. My father's birthday present, which I've been hiding away in a gray and gold present box, comes into view. The upgraded Rolex watch with a diamond-encrusted face featuring the letter A for Allen, which I ordered, came out perfect. My father has no idea that my sister and I chipped in to replace his old, flimsy Rolex, but he won't throw it out. He claims it's good luck.

I hold the box close, feeling more excited about the gift than he probably will. I glide downstairs, reaching the landing in no time, and as my foot hits the bottom step, I hear the doorbell ringing.

Walking toward the door, I see that it's Shaunie, standing there in a fire-red jumpsuit with waist-length boho twists.

I open the door excitedly. "I thought you said you weren't coming," I say, playfully punching her.

"Girl, my client canceled her appointment and said the show got delayed," she says, referring to her newest client, who is an actress.

We embrace as only sisters can, and as we walk to the backyard, I fill her in on everything that's been going on, including Uncle Charlie's unexpected appearance.

* * *

"Happy birthday to youuuuu," we all sing to my father. We crowd around him as he blows out the candles on his cake. My mother plants a large kiss on my father's forehead and looks at him in awe. I quickly wipe away a stray tear and start grabbing plates and napkins to cut pieces of cake for everyone.

My father has many friends, and I look up occasionally as hungry guests grab slices of cake. Some people have known my father his whole life, friends he's known for years, and family.

I hope that when I reach this age, I can be just as blessed.

After serving most of the guests, I grab my own plate of buttercream frosted cake and walk to the drink table, scooping up a spoonful of homemade punch. I opt to add a little extra spirit, a generous pour of cognac into my red plastic cup. After balancing the cake, drink, and my phone in both hands, I find somewhere to sit. At the table underneath our pecan tree sit my mother, Shaunie, Aunt Shirley, and Uncle Charlie, all huddled together as my father entertains his guests, playing a round of horseshoes.

"Here, come sit with us, sis," Shaunie says, pointing to the chair next to her.

Although we're all family, the table seems quiet, and we look like strangers to one another. Not even Shaunie, with her chatter about her clients, can fill this void of noise. I stuff cake into my mouth quickly, look around to avoid eye contact, and know what's coming questions.

"So, Maverick, your mother was telling us you may be home for good. Any plans on settling down soon?" my Aunt Shirley says.

I eye my mother across the table and swallow the last bit of frosting from my fork. "You know what, I'm just figuring things out, but I think my time in the Air Force is winding down, and I'm ready to try something new in my life."

"Well, that's understandable. You've been in the military long enough. It's never too late to make a change in your life," she finishes, smiling brightly at me. The way she smiles, I can tell it's genuine, and I actually don't mind her questioning me.

"Well, I say you've got a good thing going, free room and board, and you get to travel the world. You should stay as long as you can," Uncle Charlie chimes in with a sour look on his face as he turns a beer bottle upside down, making sure every drop lands in his mouth.

"Well, I say nobody asked you," my mom says defensively, coming to my rescue. I'm surprised. "And by the way, what would you know about someone working as hard as Maverick does? You haven't worked in over fifteen years." She rolls her neck and crosses her arms against her chest. The corners of her mouth scrunch up, and not even Shaunie can think of something clever to say.

"Nina, now I didn't mean anything by it. You're always ready to fight somebody."

"And you're always ready to run your mouth, Charlie."

"You know what," he says, standing. "I told Shirl not to bring me over here. Your own momma and daddy couldn't say two words to you. It's a wonder why they couldn't stand you, and I can't either."

"Oh, you want to go there?" my mom says, standing quickly too, her chair falling back from the sudden movement. "You and they can kiss my ass. They couldn't stand the fact that I didn't listen to them and paved my own way." She stands proudly, not backing down.

I'm not sure how a simple question ended up becoming this heated between my mother and Uncle Charlie. It's no wonder he never comes around. I stare across the table at Aunt Shirley as she tries to intervene and calm them both down.

"Y'all, we're family. Let's not do this. Nina, this is a special event."

"No, she wants to argue, let's go. Our parents couldn't stand that 'paving your way,'" he says, throwing up air quotes. "It meant your ass getting pregnant. You threw your life away to get knocked up. You had a full ride as the first person in our family to go to college and be somebody, but you messed it up. If they were mad about anything, it was that and the way you left your family high and dry." Speaking with finality, he sits back down, his angry face resembling my mother's.

"Charles, you've got some nerve...this coming from the same man who forfeited his career, and ain't anything ever good come from your life. But somehow your choices were forgiven, but me getting pregnant was where they were disappointed. Give me a break. So what if I chose my family? They wanted to disown me. So yeah, they weren't at the top of my list to visit. And besides, I don't have to explain myself to anyone, especially not you."

My mother's voice rises during the exchange until she's screaming. It doesn't take long for my father, who was across the yard, to make his way to my mother. He stands loyally by her side, not even asking what's going on. He takes one look at Uncle Charlie and says, "I think it's time you leave, man...let me walk you out." His voice is cool, with no evidence of worry or concern. He says his words as a matter-of-fact statement, motioning to the gate for them to exit.

Uncle Charlie opens his mouth but slowly closes it again as he walks past my father. He mumbles under his breath, but nothing loud enough to be legible. My Aunt Shirley also quickly follows, but not before mouthing I'm sorry to my mother, who is almost at the point of tears.

"Let's go inside," Shaunie says.

I follow her orders and think about what just occurred. Why was my mother coming to my defense? Why did Uncle Charlie's words disturb her so much that she was on the verge of tears? And why didn't she ever rebuild the relationship with her parents?

My head is in a storm of emotions as we walk back to the house. Most of the party goers have no idea the party was about to turn into something else. But I can tell, just by how my mother is walking with her shoulders hunched and avoiding any glares, that she is not herself.

We all sit down in the den, just letting my mother breathe for a few minutes. Shaunie, being the leader among the two of us, jumps straight into the conversation.

"Momma, Uncle Charlie was out of line, but so were you... why was he talking to you like that? I thought you said our grandparents loved the fact that when you had me, they were excited about it. Were you lying to me?"

Her face softens a little. "Baby, they did love you...but they just couldn't love me again. I broke their hearts when I became pregnant, and they and Charlie never let me forget it. It was a stain they just couldn't look past."

I timidly jump in. "But if they loved Shaunie, how come they couldn't forgive you?"

"I don't know," my mom says regretfully. "They just couldn't. My parents dropped out of school and only had an eighth-grade education. They poured a lot into Charlie and me, giving the best they got. Charlie messing up his career hurt them, but my getting pregnant at a young age broke their heart. All they ever wanted for me was an education, and when I became pregnant, that part of my life became secondary to my family." She wipes the tears falling with the back of her hand. "But I don't regret it at all...your father was the best thing to ever happen to me."

Seeming to regain her composure, she appears more in charge now as she rises from the couch and stands.

"Listen, I'm not feeling too well after all this. Tell your father I'll be upstairs for a while...You girls, clean up once all these damn people leave our house."

We both nod in acknowledgment and watch as my mom slowly walks up the stairs, carrying something, and now I finally know what it is. The guilt of having a teen pregnancy that cost her a relationship with her parents. That sounds familiar.

Shaunie and I exchange glances, but don't have time to talk, as I see my father entering the house.

"Mom's upstairs," I say quickly, knowing who he's looking for.

"Thanks, baby doll. I'll chat with her and be back down in a minute. By the way, your friend Jeremiah called and said he couldn't make it. I think it's time this party gets wrapped up. I'm tired."

He takes off up the stairs, headed to their bedroom.

After hours of cleaning up and making sure the party planner has all of her tables, chairs, and equipment, it seems it's finally the end of a tumultuous celebration. Shaunie has retired early, which is unlike her, but she mentioned being tired from her flight. My mom has been upstairs since earlier and still hasn't managed to come back downstairs. The only people up are my father and I. He's retired to the basement, his happy place. As I wipe down the kitchen counters to remove any leftover crumbs and food, I figure my dad could use some company and walk downstairs into his Clemson-fanatic man cave.

As I near the bottom of the stairs, I hear Marvin Gaye's "Mercy Mercy Me" playing on his record player. I stand at the landing, watching my father two-step to the song, a party of one.

"Hey, Dad, just seeing if you want some company?"

"Of course, baby girl, always," he says as he walks over and grabs my hand, spinning me around playfully like when I was a child.

"So what's on your mind? And don't tell me anything, you've been here a few months, and I still don't know why."

I stop dancing with him and plop down on the leather sectional. "I don't know...I guess I just had nowhere else to go. I can't really go into detail about work."

"Come on, this isn't some officer you're talking to, it's your dad. Tell me what's really going on. You know I understand military theatrics and just how tough things are."

I contemplate being vague and lying, but as I stare into my father's eyes, I know the truth is what I need to say. No longer can the things left unsaid carry such heavy weight in my heart.

"I...um...I made a mistake, one that can't be easily forgotten. I got involved with another officer of mine and discovered some things I shouldn't have about him. We were dating, but I found out he was lying to me about pursuing a relationship and about work. When I confronted him with my superior in the room, he still lied. I had no way to prove what he was lying about, and because of it, I lost my spot."

My father looks on with a range of emotions from disappointment and fear to relief as I explain to him what happened.

"And that's the real reason I'm home: they wanted to demote me, and instead, I requested a leave of absence. I'm not sure what I want to do now, whether to go back...or start something new. But all I've ever done is work on drones and such."

"Oh, baby girl...is that it? You just made a mistake. Now, the main thing is you've got to let this person, whoever he is, go. A person like that, one who will go to that extreme to be dishonest, either has a bad heart or a good reason; either way, he doesn't deserve you. You're going to figure this out, baby." He sits down next to me and rubs my shoulder. The sigh of relief I exhale lets a heavy weight roll out of me. Someone in my family knows the truth and hasn't judged me or made me feel small.

"Now, baby...we have to tell your mama and Shaunie?"

My shoulders slump slightly. I'd been avoiding telling them out of fear of the questions they would ask.

"Yeah, I know. It's time I stop keeping so much to myself. They deserve to know how I'm doing...and not just some front or excuse."

"You're right about that. This family has enough secrets...we don't need any more."

"What do you mean?"

"You know we just have enough going on, is all I'm saying." My father looks away timidly. My instincts tell me there's more he wants to say. I've never known my father to be timid. Not sure what I'm pressing for, I keep asking.

"Really, Dad, what are you talking about?"

"Listen, it's late. Maybe you should just lie down. I've had enough whiskey tonight."

Growing more alarmed but trying to hide it, I ask him one last question.

"Is this about what happened tonight with Mama and Uncle Charlie?"

"No, baby, just honestly forget I even said anything."

"OK," I say, shifting my mind. I walk over to the tall bookcase my father has, holding his military accomplishments, family photos, and souvenirs from his travels. My eyes settle on a picture of him and my Grandmother Clarisse. He's sitting between her legs on the front porch of his childhood home. I pick up the picture from its frame, and memories of my Gammy flood my brain.

I sure do miss my Grandma Clarisse; she knew how to party and could always magically make people get along.

My father walks over and marvels at the photo, unlocking a core memory of the moment the picture was taken. "Yes, she sure could...You know, before she died, she always talked about you. She used to say that, underneath that tough wall of yours, you had a big heart...just needed the right person to tend to it. She was so proud of you, and for the life of me, I could never get her to stop trying to put a child on you." He laughs excitedly, placing the photo back down.

Instead of meeting his laughter, a feeling of unease creeps into my chest, and I can't match his smile. But instead of letting nerves and my emotions spiral, I take another deep breath, ready to get serious.

"What do you mean by that?" I ask, unsure, but deep in my stomach, I know there's more.

"Well, one day I went to visit her, it had to have been almost five years ago, right before her health started failing. We talked, and I distinctly remember her asking me, 'Where is Mav's son?' And I remember thinking maybe she was confusing you with someone." He pauses, smiling at the thought of her. "She was so persistent that day...she just kept asking where he was."

My eyes brim with tears as I think back to the day my mom was on the phone, the day she found out I was pregnant, and I never knew she was talking to my grandmother. I blink back my tears, but they still manage to land on my cheek.

"So anyway," my dad resumes, "I told her she was confusing you with someone else, you never had a child. I kept repeating it to her until she really heard me, but in my eyes, she never did. She was adamant, and when she finally responded, she said the baby was in heaven."

So she knew too. I thought only Mom and I would die with that secret, but I guess I was wrong. You both knew. A pressure in the pit of my stomach releases. I don't know if I feel more relieved knowing my secret is out in the open or embarrassed that I never said anything.

"So you knew...the whole time you knew what she made me do? And you never said anything?" I look at my dad sitting in his leather recliner, a whiskey glass in one hand.

His lids seem heavy as he blinks back wetness from his eyes, but I know no tears will fall, because that's just the type of man he is. His eyes keep staring in my direction, but not at me; it's like he's looking beyond me somehow.

"I...I knew one day that you wouldn't be my little girl anymore. From the day you were born, a time would come when you wouldn't be mine anymore, but the world's." He pauses, clinking the ice cubes against the glass before taking a drink.

"Your mother never told me, and for all purposes, I never told her I knew. Your Grandmother Clarisse could never quite keep a secret. Do you remember when your grandmother started to have problems with her memory?"

I shake my head yes, thinking of my grandmother, affectionately known as Gammy, who later began showing signs of dementia.

My father continues. "I don't know all the ins and outs, but I know your mother, and she wouldn't let this happen. Even though I don't agree with how she handled it, I know it was to protect you."

"What do you mean, protect me?" I say, projecting my voice, but quickly lowering it again.

"Mav, baby, you don't know what type of choices your mother had to make. We got pregnant, and your mom's family almost disowned her. You saw that tonight...those still waters run deep, and her family was never the same. She didn't want you to repeat what she did."

I stare down at my lap, processing what my father said. She didn't want me to be like her. I made the same mistakes she did. She thought she was doing what was right.

I continue staring at my empty palms. "I understand that better now...but during that time, it felt like she was embarrassed by my choices. And I didn't know what I wanted to do...but she took away my option. It was still my right to decide." My eyes boil with fresh tears.

My father consoles me as the tears continue to spill onto my cheek, and onto his hand as he gently wipes them away.

"I know, baby. I know everything's going to be fine."

Chapter 3: Healing

Abruptly leaving Seoul meant being shipped out before undergoing surgery for my fibroid. My temporary medical leave would soon run out. I wanted the reality of having something wrong within me to be left behind, but once I returned to Charleston, my pain became too hard to hide. In less than three months, my periods went from barely manageable to outright hell. I even sought second and third opinions, and each doctor gave me the same answer: I need surgery.

My body attacks itself, and the price I pay is a tormented womb. In a way, our bodies always keep score and alert us to a problem. Between stress and embarrassment, I've been getting my fair share of emotional pain. But to have the physical pain attack me feels like an uppercut to my gut.

Last month, I had the worst pain I'd ever experienced. I did my usual routine, preparing myself for the worst as my cycle approached. I tried blocking out the immeasurable discomfort I felt. The two spare bottles of Tylenol I kept on my nightstand, along with old reruns on TV, kept me preoccupied as I prepared not to get out of bed for the day.

But my false sense of comfort came to an end when I felt an overwhelming gush of blood between my legs. Reaching my hands under the light blanket that was draped across my body,

I felt down below, realizing blood was now on my sheets and my right hand.

I sat on the edge of the bed, balancing on the tips of my toes against the rug beneath my feet, standing up achingly slow. Each lurch I made toward the door felt like my uterus could fall out right onto the floor. Stumbling into the upstairs hallway, I grip the stair railing, trying to maintain my balance. The pain is so heavy, my body is tired. I am tired.

I can't contain it. My feet trip, and to the ground I go. All I can do is hug myself right there on the floor, not even bothering to call for help. The fuzzy pink pajama bottoms I'm wearing have turned crimson along the seams of my crotch. Exhausted, I close my eyes as the pain radiates from my core.

I come to with gentle swipes against my cheek, and for just a moment, I think it's Jun Pyo rubbing me so tenderly. But when I open my eyes, I see it's my mother's hands I feel. Sitting up quickly, trying to recover, feels futile as the pain in my abdomen returns.

"Just lie back, Mavvy. Mom's got you," she says. I can tell her eyes are strained and cloudy. She's been crying.

I lean up again, this time using my elbows to prop myself up and steady my breathing.

"Mom, I'm okay. You know it's just the fibroid. I've been having some intense pain this month. I didn't realize it would take this much out of me," I say quickly, wiping my brow, now slick with sweat.

"I just need to get up and shower for a bit...I'll be fine."

"I say you should go to the hospital; there's no telling what's really going on with your body."

I look at her strangely before responding. She hasn't shown this much attention to my body since I was seventeen. The care and concern seem oddly familiar, yet also out of place coming from her. I want to shrug off her suggestion, but passing out is not normal for me, and this pain continues to intensify.

But against my mother's wishes, I coax myself up slowly, leaning on the stair railing to gather my strength.

"I'm going to get some rest for now. I just need to be alone." I can tell her feelings are hurt as she looks down at the ground, her face sunken.

I walk toward the bathroom to get cleaned up, and even the small task of taking off my clothes to get in the shower feels strenuous. After placing the blood-soaked pajama bottoms in the trash can, I turn on the faucet, letting the water run as hot as possible. It isn't until the mirrors are steamed and the bathroom temperature has risen a few degrees that I finally step into the shower.

The streams of water pour down onto me, and I grip the tiled wall as another shock wave of pain hits. I muster my strength and clench my teeth, my jaw locked tight, as a huge clot escapes down the drain and my eyes close. I can't do this anymore.

On cue, I hear a light knock at the door.

"Hey, Mav, I'm outside the door, but if you need any help, I'm right here."

I'd prefer anyone else, but my mom helps me; she's all I've got in this moment. In my time of need, she's the one I have to lean on.

"Come in," I say. I hear the door open and close quickly. Then I add, "I need help getting a towel and some pads, please."

"Alright, baby, whatever you need, I've got you."

The sense of closeness I feel is unusual for her to show this level of care. My heart beats loudly, and even though I've got clothes on again, something feels heavy in my chest from exhaustion. I feel like I'm about to pass out again, and this time, instead of being hardheaded, I take my mother's advice.

"I need to go to the doctor, Mommy." I hate the way I sound like a little child, but deep down, I feel a pain and uncertainty only a mother can calm with the reassurance of her voice.

"I've got you, baby...I've got you." My mother rubs my head, standing above me as I sit on the toilet, easing the weakness in my legs.

* * *

It's been twelve hours since my admittance to the hospital, and my mom hasn't left my side yet. Being admitted has been a wake-up call. According to the doctors who have been examining me, I lost a significant amount of blood and was hemorrhaging. They said I was lucky to have even made it to the hospital without bleeding more.

My mother and father have been watching me like hawks, barely leaving my bedside as I'm given blood and fluids through an IV. Looking up at the clock on the wall, it's about eleven-thirty p.m., and my parents are sprawled across a small recliner and pull-out bed, sleeping peacefully. I can't believe it took almost dying to really see a mother instead of someone I hated for years. I guess that's probably what she feels, too.

A light knock sounds at the door, and night-shift Nurse Jameson walks in, humming a familiar song I can't quite place. But as soon as she opens her mouth, I hear the thick Gullah accent trying to leap through.

Hey, Ms. Maverick, just checking in on you before I make my rounds.

I'm doing better...but ready to go home.

It'll be soon enough, but let me check your vitals and get you another IV drip bag, baby.

Thank you, I say. As she bends down over me, straightening some cords that have become tangled, I notice a pretty beaded bracelet with miniature conch shells on it. "So, are you from the Low country?"

Gullah, to be specific, she says, smiling, "but my family is also from Jamaica, so I've got a little bit of both. Though I thought my accent had disappeared since I've been here so long."

It's very faint…But I can still tell it's there. "Where did you grow up?"

Mainly the Edisto Islands…I have some family there. They thought I was crazy for becoming a nurse working in this field when they believed in natural healing." She laughs to herself, as if recounting a memory.

But I'll have to save that story for another time…do you need anything else?

I believe I'll be fine, thank you, Jameson….

Oh, honey, call me Fran…see you soon.

Fran, see you soon. I smile wholeheartedly as she exits the room, closing my eyes to try and rest.

It's almost afternoon when I finally open my eyes, surprised that I've been sleeping this long. My parents aren't in the spot I saw them in a few hours ago, but I know they're probably not far. As the silence of my room sinks in, the depth of what I'm missing in this moment plagues my mind and heart, the fear of possibly dying and not having a soul to help me had I been by myself. No emergency contact. No one to check on me.

Had this happened overseas, I could have experienced a different fate. But instead, I'm in Charleston, in this room, with IVs plugged into my arms because I decided to put off taking care of my body. The remorse and weight of my disregard for my health make me feel like an elephant is sitting on my chest. I've got to do better at prioritizing my health.

The door opens, and instantly the noise of other patient monitors and chatting fills the room.

"Hello, Maverick...are you decent? This is Doctor Shaw. May I enter?"

I straighten my gown lightly, making sure I'm not showing too much flesh as Dr. Shaw enters. He's a middle-aged white man with a bald head, hazel eyes, and a big smile that never ceases to amaze me.

So happy you're up, and I heard you're feeling much better today. I presume you're itching to get out of here. Am I right?

I smile, trying to match his easygoing smile and words. "Yes, Dr. Shaw, please tell me I can go home."

Wonderful. Well, I will clear you to go home later today, but we need to have a serious talk about your next steps. His lighthearted voice becomes heavier as he slides an examining stool near the bed and speaks to me at eye level.

My chest tightens, anticipating the worst and feeling reluctant to receive any good news.

Maverick, take a deep breath. I promise it's going to be okay.

I am still reluctant, but I take a deep breath, trying to push the anxiety I feel down my throat.

Now, I want to first say you were extremely lucky to get help when you did. I know you've suffered through these pains for a long time, but as you get older, your body may not be able to keep experiencing the adverse effects of the cysts in your womb. The bleeding needs to be managed. Surgery is possible, but these cysts can recur. And if they block your ovarian tubes, we could be looking at permanent damage. I know this isn't what you want, but I would strongly encourage you to think about it.

My eyes swell with tears instantly. Here we go again.

My release from the hospital feels like a blur. I was still too weak to stand, and I was wheeled out by my father and escorted to his pickup truck. Ever since the news from the doctor, something in me has gone numb...my heart feels just as weak as my body. Something in me stirs as we pull up to my parents' house. And although I have no recollection of how we got here, my hands reach quickly for the door handle, and I just want to crawl into a hole.

Hey there, baby, take it easy...let me help you get out, my dad says.

I wait for him to exit the car, and I hear my mother behind me open the door as well. She collects my hospital bag of items and unlocks the screen door, leaving it open for my father and me.

He gently helps me hop down from the truck and places my feet slowly, one foot in front of the other. The slow, concerted effort by both my parents to be gentle with me is apparent; they are treating me like a fragile piece of crystal, and I can tell their brave faces are sinking. They overheard Doctor Shaw's news and fully know all my health secrets I've tried to hide. The relief I feel is small in comparison to the fear I feel of having to get surgery that doesn't even stop the attack on my body permanently.

My mind races as I take a step toward the staircase to my room, but my mother interjects.

"Actually, we thought you'd be more comfortable in the guest room, at least for a few days. I've fixed it up for you."

Thank you, that was very sweet of you.

I take my time walking to the small guest room our family used when family would come from out of town. I stroll toward the door, staring at the beige comforter and small desk with my mother's sewing machine sitting beside the bed. I relax as my parents stand in the doorway.

We'll leave you to it. Call us if you need any help, my father says, grabbing my mother's hand and walking away. But before she turns to leave, my mother reaches into her back pocket.

Nurse Jameson wanted to say goodbye, but couldn't make it. She did want to give you her phone number.

She passes me a small scrap of paper. Fran Jameson, 843 524 9542. Thanks, I'll give her a call.

I pick up the phone lying next to me and dial the number silently, thinking about what makes me so special to Nurse Jameson that she gave me her number. The line rings a few times, and I almost hang up, but just as I pull the phone away from my ear, I hear Fran with her rich accent.

Hello, this is Fran speaking.

Hi, Nurse Jameson, this is Maverick Robinson. My mother mentioned that you gave her your number for me to contact you. I just wanted to follow up and let you know I have made it home safely.

Oh, sweetie, this is great news. I know you were in the hospital for a short time, but I enjoyed caring for you.

Thank you, you took great care of me. Feeling flattered yet uneasy about what else I should say, the line grows quiet in awkward silence.

Well, I wanted to say goodbye, but I also wanted to chat with you...Before I say anything, I just want to tell you I mean no offense by what I'm about to say.

OK, I say, nodding my head as if she's in the room with me.

Now I know the doctor talked about possible surgery, but I wanted to walk you through some more options. Even though I work in the healthcare field, there are certain things Western medicine will just never understand about authentic healing, especially for a woman.

I remain quiet, still unsure of what Nurse Jameson wants to tell me.

Have you considered the surgery?

Feeling my chest tighten just at the mention of surgery again, I clear my throat. I was told to get surgery before when I was abroad, but I don't want to do it if it means I can never have children, I say bluntly.

I understand that. If I'm not being too forward, I would suggest there's another option. I know firsthand what it feels like to have a fibroid, and it's hell. I was very close to electing to have surgery about two years ago, but my family persuaded me not to. I was scared about not being able to conceive, and even worse, the fear that it would come back.

Wow, I didn't know...it feels refreshing to speak with someone who's been through this before. But you said you didn't get the surgery, so what did you do instead? Are you still sick? The words rush out of my mouth like fire from a water hose.

I am not sick, thank Jesus, but it took me a while to find a process that works for me. I went the holistic route and never looked back. My people believe we have all the medicine we need right here from the earth...the herbs are healing.

I'm not sure what you mean, Fran...I've heard of herbal tea, but I never knew any of that stuff actually worked.

It does, you just have to know what to use. Look, I'm going to text you where I go in town to get what I need. There's a flea market off Collins Road that has been around forever. Go there, and a little old lady selling jewels and the right herbs will be there. I promise you will feel ten times better.

Still unsure but open to trying anything other than surgery, I hesitate, then agree, to visit the flea market this weekend. After wrapping up briefly with Fran and thanking her for her help, I lay back on the bed, staring at the ceiling. I need healing, I whisper to an empty room, touching my stomach.

* * *

The flea markets in Charleston are the best places to find fresh vegetables, seafood, and fruit. From merchants selling holistic herbs and traditional Gullah staples, you can find anything here. Collins Road was one of the longest-standing markets, dating back to the early 1900s. The market now consists mostly of farmers and local retailers. But back in its origins, enslaved people were traded here, brought off boats from Europe. Not many remnants remain, except for a statue with inscriptions. A small native boy and a tall man with a telescope stand there, made of fine pieces of metal, carved to overlook the market. They are pointing northward toward the street. The man, Horace Collins, helped map the island, but according to locals, he also tried to take its culture.

I pass stall after stall, each offering a colorful selection of imaginable products, in search of the woman Fran told me about. A woman with beautiful silver locks and brown skin smiles and waves me over to her table, wearing a flowing dress that stops at the tops of her feet. She's talking, and I can hear the deep Gullah accent spill out as she points me toward the colorful jewelry on the table. Bracelets, earrings, and necklaces sit on display stands. There are golden rings with topaz and jasmine stones, and a small necklace with a stone the color of the ocean that catches my attention. I thumb it over my fingers, debating if I want to buy it. But before I can keep looking, the lady ushers me closer, grabbing my forearm and showing me more of her inventory.

At a table set further back from the aisle, she walks me to one filled with unique herbs and natural remedies. I pick up the small bags of herbs, smelling each one: lavender, lemongrass, and citrus. Curious to know what the herbs are good for, I ask, "I like the lemongrass herb...what does it help with?"

This one is good for your pain and makes you really strong.

I keep examining the table, picking up something else I'm not familiar with. "And this one dandelion root looks like a flower?"

The woman smiles at my curiosity and responds, "It's the flower to help with women's issues. It cleans your body and purifies you. If you drink it at least twice a week, you will notice a difference. This makes the men come to you, and your skin will be glowing."

I smile at her charm, figuring this is the herb lady Fran mentioned.

"It cleans the womb." Her smile widens as she grabs the bag of dandelion root and places it in a small pouch. "Here, try it for free, and you come back and tell me if it works."

Surprised and grateful, I try to reach for a few dollars in my wallet to give to her, but she refuses. "Tek Um," she says, her thick Geechee phrase spilling out naturally. I smile politely before thanking her again and continuing my trek through the farmers' market.

Growing up in Charleston meant having a deep fascination with the culture. I remember being a child and traveling to museums that did their best to explain the impact the Atlantic slave trade had on the people here. I still see the disparity in the city, noticing how much remains segregated. But the Gullah people somehow found a way to keep their land, traditions, and culture on their islands. I can't seem to be filled with anything but hope and expectation as I stare down at the bag of herbs.

I look forward to giving this a try instead of getting surgery to have my fibroid removed. My research has me second-guessing whether it's even a real option to avoid surgery, based on the sheer pain it causes every month without removal. But looking at the numbers, just because I have the surgery doesn't mean they won't grow back. I guess I'll try the holistic route; it feels like something I can at least explore.

As I place my small items into the bike I've rented for the day to navigate uptown, my stomach growls loudly. I consider heading home, but I end up catching the most amazing smell as I unlock the bike from a light pole in front of the farmers' market. The aroma drifts from across the street at Geechee Plate, a local Gullah restaurant. My mouth waters as I realize it's been far too long since I've eaten there. My hunger leads the way as I lock the bike back up and grab my small bag from the farmers' market.

Geechee Plate is one of the oldest restaurants in town and has been around since I was a kid. Although it's a locals' spot, the restaurant also attracts tourists since it's within walking distance of Charleston's famous riverfront. After walking inside, I'm pleasantly surprised to see a few tables available, and sitting down feels promising.

"Excuse me, miss, how many?" a female waitress asks.

"Just one."

"All right then, follow me."

The waitress seats me at a table by the wall, lined with portraits of the Gullah people and traditional dishes. I spend the first few minutes simply admiring all the history these walls hold. My eyes scan the menu, looking for something familiar and hearty. The fried green tomatoes, grits, and crab cakes sound delicious. I wait patiently until the waitress returns, humming softly to the music playing overhead.

My mind wanders, and I catch myself wondering what Jun Pyo is up to, what he's doing at this exact moment. I quickly push the thought to the back of my mind, trying to forget the last year of my life.

"Excuse me, miss, are you ready to order?"

"Yes, I'll take the grits, green tomatoes, and crab cakes. And a coffee black, no cream."

"Will anyone be joining you today?" she asks, glancing at the empty chair across from me.

"No, I'm by myself."

Chapter 4: Take Me to Church

It's Sunday, and unlike the last three Sundays, when I woke up at noon and lounged in pajamas, hiding out in my room, I am up fully dressed in my Sunday best. Per my father's request, he wants us all to go to church as a family. My two-piece lavender suit with breast pockets accentuates my bust line, as I opt for a simple white tank top, anticipating the spring heat. With light makeup, a high bun, and leopard print heeled mules, I look good.

The way I admire myself in the mirror gives me a flashback to the old me. My insides quiver at the thought of crossing the threshold of Ame Zion Hilltop Church. My parents had been members there since I was a child. Shaunie and I grew up there; she had her first kiss with Pastor Woodbine's son behind the piano organ. I had my first fistfight on stage while performing in the Easter play, after Cordelia Johnson tried to take my solo.

The church held fond memories from my childhood. But during the time I had the abortion, I stopped believing. My mother always pushed me afterward, telling me to go, but knowing the truth, she never pushed me too hard. Growing up, my father was a devout couch potato most Sundays. He only showed up for funerals, Easter, Christmas, and Mother's Day once he retired from the military. But a few years ago, something just clicked, and he went to church without my mother begging him to go.

The last Sunday I was in a church was over ten years ago. But this morning, this day, I would go into the House of the Lord, as my grandmother would say. It was the first Sunday of the month, Resurrection Sunday. That meant instead of leaving in two hours, it would be closer to three. I stared down at my watch, debating whether I should stay home instead. But the doubt and escape plan disappeared as I saw my father standing in my doorway.

"Mav, baby doll, you ready?" he says, coaxing me.

I look back at him. He's dressed sharply in a signature gray suit, with Opal Stacey Adams shoes. Considering myself as someone who never disappoints my father, I grab a small clutch off the dresser and follow him down the stairs.

"Take me to church," I say in a fake but enthusiastic tone.

I sit in the passenger seat of my father's Chevy pickup truck as we make a left onto Baker Street a long road that passes a cemetery, a few houses, and a fire station, leading to the church. My mother conveniently doesn't feel well, so she stayed home. Although I think she's sick because she doesn't want to be seen in church with me, having to answer all the questions of why I haven't been to church in so long, or why I'm even home. She's always been like that, caring too much about what others thought. With the windows down and the sky Carolina blue, I tap my finger on the window seal as we draw nearer.

Ame Zion Hilltop was a medium-sized church, not quite a megachurch, but the congregation was well over two hundred people. The outside driveway led to a large parking lot to the right. A maple tree, wide enough for my arms to hug, was settled near the road with a welcome sign. The grassy knolls where I used to play after church were now filled with yellow daisies and purple lilac flowers. You could see them from the road, along with a large cross at the front of a wooden entry. Almost majestic were the two large doors that welcomed you into the sanctuary. Squinting my eyes, I could see the glass reflection of rainbow hues inside as someone walked in.

Taking a deep breath, I unclasped my seat belt as my father did his as well. We were early, not just ten minutes early, but with enough time to find a seat. We were at least an hour early for church. The parking lot was almost bare, except for a few other cars.

Did we have to come this early?

Yes, Maverick. I told you I have to help usher this morning. Come on, ain't no sense in sitting here.

Knowing not to question my father, I exited the car quickly. I already felt like taking my blazer off, as the sun's warmth on my skin made me want to take it off. I strolled behind him as we walked through the main entrance. I scanned the church; the main hall still had a corkscrew board filled with events, fundraisers, and prayers for those who were sick. The decor was still the same: a floral accent couch sat in front of the women's bathroom, which was powder pink. I quietly motioned to my father that I was heading that way as he started talking to another usher.

Walking diagonally into the bathroom, I stood in front of the mirror, admiring myself but looking for something deeper than admiration. I've got a thing for mirrors, I guess. They say the eyes are the windows to your soul, and I think mirrors are too. It was a reflecting glass. Applying a layer of red matte lipstick, I smoothed my lavender skirt, making sure it sat just right, not too high above my knees. But somehow, since coming back home, my hips and thighs had spread in the skirt, which hugged my behind, making the skirt rise. With one final glance, I stepped out of the bathroom to find my father.

I didn't expect much to happen today; church had never been my thing as an adult, and it had been an obligation as a child. But I braced myself, grabbing the door handle to exit.

I've got this.

The church service so far had consisted of squeezed cheeks from church mothers who had reserved seats in the first three pews. My father had introduced me to at least four single men who loved the Lord and had offered to show me around town. I refused, to my father's dismay. We were seated close enough to hear the pastor speaking. He started talking about forgiving oneself. His words struck a chord deep within the confines of my soul, and suddenly, all my attention was on him.

Now, church, we know what it's like to disappoint God through our choices and mistakes. But the Word says that God forgives us, so why can't we forgive ourselves?

My heart jumped into my stomach, recalling all the times I'd messed up. All the time that had passed, where I never permitted myself to extend grace, an overwhelming feeling of surrender and freedom flooded my body. The only thing I could do to let some of the anguish and guilt out was to cry, and slowly, tears slid down. Bending my head down low between my legs, the tears stained my pants, but I didn't care.

I feel alone.

But just as I bent down lower so no one could see these tears, I felt a hand on my shoulder. It was my father, standing there with tissues in his hands. I reached for them, wiping my eyes.

I am not alone this time.

The chords within my heart opened up, and I continued

listening.

The pastor continued, "It doesn't matter what you've done. God says that He forgives the sins of those who seek repentance. It doesn't matter that you fornicated. It doesn't matter that you came to God and failed at keeping your promises. It doesn't matter that you didn't keep the baby and got an abortion in the past. It doesn't matter that your past is not pretty. What matters is that this is your chance to reestablish your relationship with God right now. All those in need of prayer, come to the altar; don't wait."

I get up out of my seat without even thinking and walk down like some sort of possessed being. The liberation I feel can't be compared to anything as I walk down the aisle to the front of the church. My father is still by my side, now holding my hand. I can't recall ever feeling so free, and all I can do is cry. As if on cue, the sun's rays shine through the large stained glass window, its rainbow of colors spilling down on me. I can't say I'm a born-again Christian, but I do know the shackles of my past won't keep me stuck any longer. From this day forward, I won't I can't look back. My life goes on with no regrets.

I cross the threshold to my parents' house, taking off my heels and feeling a new sense of hope. My father has dropped me off as he enjoys a few rounds of golf with some friends from a veteran group he attends. The house is quiet, and the patio door is open to the deck. I can hear the faint sound of music playing in the background. I walk toward the door, peeking my head out to speak to my mother, who couldn't make it to church. Although she had claimed to be sick, she looked surprisingly well, sipping from a mason jar, an ice-cold cup of sweet tea.

"Made it back. Daddy said he's going to play golf." I don't wait for a response and figure I'll just head upstairs, but my mother stops me.

"Mav... I think it's time we talk." She looks sincere, and ever since I got sick, she's acted like a mother more in the last few weeks than in the last ten years. But I'm still unsure if my wounds and trust can be restored just because of what she's done lately.

"Let me change out of these clothes, and I'll join you."

I head toward my room and couldn't care less about changing my clothes, but I buy myself some time as I slip on a house gown and flip flops, making myself more comfortable. I can count on my hands how many serious conversations my mother has initiated with me. She's not much of a talker; she likes to boss people around until they do what she tells them. Her favorite saying growing up was, "When I talk, you follow," her phrase for no nonsense whenever my sister or I wanted to question a command of hers. She wasn't a horrible mother, but for some reason, she never let her guard down with us. It seemed my father was the only one who could reach, deter, and let down those walls she had built.

Taking my time walking back out toward the deck, I pour myself a glass of lemonade before going back out. I sit adjacent to her on the wooden rocking chair with the engraving "R" for our family name. The cold glass of lemonade makes my body feel cooler, but inside, there's a heap of anxiety about what this conversation will hold.

"What do you want to talk about?"

"Your father told me about things at church. He called me after the service and said there were some things I needed to say and tell you. And so I want to... I want to clear the air. We both know that over these years, we have been like oil and water. We don't mix." She takes a deep breath and twirls her thumbs between her fingers, a nervous habit of hers.

"I want to say I'm sorry... deeply sorry for making you get rid of your child. I was afraid of what people would say, but more than anything, I was terrified that you'd turn out like me. I always wanted my children to be better than I am." She pulls a piece of her gray hair behind her ear, looking unsure of what to say. But she's not getting off easily. I need more.

Thank you for telling me that, but I need more. That decision was one of the hardest things I have ever had to deal with. To this day, I think about that child and wonder how my life would've been. I need more answers.

My mother looks around, hesitant, as if someone might overhear us. The woman I've dreamed up in my mind seems so small in front of me.

"I... uhmm... Your father and I never told you and Shaunie, but I was pregnant once before. Your father knew, and we decided not to go through with it. My parents found out soon after and told me it was your father or them. I had to choose. In that time, it wasn't common down here to have children out of wedlock. I couldn't imagine my family had high expectations for us."

I look on, horrified, at the thought of my parents having a child even younger than I was. Placing my hand over my mouth, I continue to listen to my mother.

"They always thought I would be the one to make it because of how smart I was. And I believed it, but I loved your father too much. We were both kids and didn't expect things to happen so quickly, but we knew we couldn't keep it a secret.

Your father wasn't old enough to join the military at that time, and I couldn't just quit school. We waited again, but Shaunie soon came. We thought we were careful enough, but we weren't. My parents were forgiving when I decided not to have the first baby, but to go through with the second was unforgivable to them. Your father tried his best to appease my parents, but they couldn't stand him. His family didn't have any money, and he wasn't going to college; they believed I was throwing my future away. It's haunted me that my last words to my parents weren't on their deathbed, but decades ago in arguments and yells. I can never get that time back."

Tears slide down my mother's face as she reaches, pushing her hair away from her face and fanning herself.

"I didn't want what happened to me to be the same type of fate you had. I'd rather you hate me and live a life worth living than be like me."

My mother's words leave me feeling confused. The compassion and hurt I feel for her and my father engorge me and bring a familiar heat to my face as it flushes. But there's something else brewing that I need to get out in this conversation. To truly heal, I have to get some things off my chest so we can finally move past this.

"I want to say first that I appreciate everything you shared with me. I empathize with your story, and as a mother, I understand you just wanted to look out for me. But you taking my decision away has impacted me in ways you don't know. Our relationship never felt the same after that happened. I needed my mother. I needed you to tell me we could figure it out. I needed you to tell me I didn't make the biggest mistake of my life. There have been so many times when you have challenged me, ridiculed me, and made me feel small. You say you want me to be better than you, but you never let me forget that I don't have what you force-feed into what my life should look like. I'm not saying all of this to hurt you, but this is our truth. I don't know if we'll ever be close like I envisioned, but I'm willing to forgive and try to make amends."

My mother shakes her head, humbly taking in everything I've said.

"I will respect you as my mother and not be so easily offended, as long as you agree to stay out of my business and stop asking me about husbands and grandbabies."

"I can do that," she says, shaking her head quickly.

"All right, then give me a hug, Mom."

We both stand and embrace as the moments pass. I feel my soul stirring, and something inside says everything will be OK.

II

Part Two

Chapter 5: Silver Bullet

My father saw me leaving early in the morning, and I explained to him that I was going to see a friend. But who I'm seeing isn't exactly that. Violetta Stone is somewhere between an ally and a cautionary tale. I saw a recent interview and noticed that her trial will begin soon. It seems the media coverage has started back up as the first anniversary of her arrest approaches.

The sun shines through the peaking blinds of my hotel room. The drive to Chesapeake, Virginia, has somehow cleared my mind, with little traffic and few stops. I fueled up the Toyota Camry I had rented and hit the road. It's only 6 a.m., and my scheduled ambush isn't until 11, after Violetta's scheduled public appearance at the Chesapeake courthouse. My fingers roam the hotel coffee table, pouring small creamer packets into a coffee mug full of fresh coffee. A knock at the door stops me from adding the third pack of sugar to my mug. It must be room service with my breakfast order. I open the door quickly, not even looking through the peephole before turning the knob.

Instead of being greeted by room service, the hallway is deathly empty, and when I look down at the gray carpet, there's a small item glinting from the floor, along with what appears to be a postcard. I bend down quickly, analyzing the hallway to see if anyone is watching, but there's no one in sight. My index fingers trail over the bright blue postcard that reads, "Welcome to Virginia." And the shiny item in my hand … is a bullet. Its gold sheen reflects the fluorescent light. I rub it between my index finger and thumb. I flip the postcard over in my hands, reading the writing on the back, but there's nothing there. The card doesn't have anyone's name on it. …

* * *

It's now well past lunchtime, and I hear my stomach growl loudly, proof that getting a hand-delivered note with a bullet is enough to disturb your appetite. I'm parked outside the law office of Violetta's defense attorney. There is nothing out of the ordinary about the businesses that line the street. A sign for Spencer Law Services is centered between a coffee shop and a copy and print services business.

After parking, I make my way to the front door, ready to speak with Mr. Spencer. My futile attempt to see Violetta at the courthouse failed because I lacked authorization. But with a little luck, I was able to find out who her lawyer was and look up his address online. That's how I ended up at 341 Toliver Street.

The entry to the building feels like something out of an old detective movie. As I near the entrance, I notice a camera recording my every movement and a small buzzer next to the door handle. Pressing the intercom button, I wait for someone to speak, but instead I hear only the buzz of the door, indicating it's unlocked.

I walk into the quaint office, which looks nicer on the inside than it does on the outside. The lounge area features an expensive looking butterscotch colored couch. There's an older Black woman who is heavyset, and square-rimmed glasses hang off her face; she fills the room with a quiet but judgmental presence. Her lips are painted a deep red, with black liner on the edges, and I can't tell if she's angry or simply has a resting expression of disdain. Still, I walk up to the desk she's sitting at, and just as I get there, her phone rings, and she answers quickly before it can ring twice.

"Spencer Law Services, please hold," she says briskly, with a hint of sass. I doubt the person even said "yes" to being put on hold before she pressed the button.

"Hello, dear, give me a moment to take this call. In the meantime, have a seat." She doesn't wait for me to respond and goes back to the call.

I sit down and observe the office, taking in all the photos and headlines on the wall, which feature different cases the law firm has covered. There's even a picture of who I assume to be Mr. Spencer shaking hands with the city of Chesapeake's mayor. He's not too bad on the eyes, with a bald head and a salt-and-pepper goatee. My eyes move back toward the desk, and even though I'm trying to mind my business, I can't help but overhear how the front desk receptionist is speaking. She is curt and quick with whoever is on the phone and hangs up abruptly.

"Miss, how can I help you?"

"Hi, Miss," I say, pausing, hoping she'll tell me her name.

"It's Mrs. Yes, continue, young lady. How can we help you?" Even though she sounds professional, something about her tone makes me feel like I'm a student and she's a teacher.

I continue, "I would like to speak to Mr. Spencer regarding Violetta Stone."

She rudely interrupts me. "And do you have an appointment scheduled with him?"

"No, I was just hoping to have a chat with him. I need to see Violetta about"

"No appointment means no visit. I'm sorry, young lady, but you can't just show up at this place of business without an appointment."

"Look, I've traveled a long way just to see this particular person. I can help her, but I need to speak with her first. Now, I understand I don't have an appointment. Does Mr. Spencer have any availability today?"

She clicks some keys loudly on her keyboard, looking extremely uninterested, her face scrunched up. After a few moments of silence, she looks up over her monitor and smiles, taking some type of pleasure in what she's about to say.

"Let me take your information down."

I write my name on a legal pad and add a few details about why I need to contact Violetta. There's just enough to be vague but intriguing, enough to ensure Mr. Spencer has to call me.

"Mr. Spencer is not free today ... and it appears he won't be free until sometime next week. Can I schedule you then?"

"No, that's too late. I will not be in town for long ... but could you at least ask him first? I must speak to his client."

"I'm sorry, no appointment, no meeting," she says smugly.

Feeling annoyed and a little defeated, I say, "Just forget it. I'll find another way."

As I turn, I hear the door to an office open, and a loud, booming voice cuts through the room.

"Ruby, have you seen the Crawford file? I need to get ready for the deposition... Oh, I'm sorry; I didn't realize we had a guest."

"We don't. She was actually just leaving and will need to schedule an appointment."

"Ruby," he says, raising his eyebrows at her.

"Actually, I'm here to discuss Violetta Stone. I must speak to her as soon as possible."

Ruby introduces us quickly, like she knows everything about me and isn't just copying the information I wrote down a few seconds ago.

"Travis, meet Maverick Robinson. She recently returned from overseas for military work. She claims she wants to be added to Violetta's approved visitation list."

My eyes lock onto the deep baritone voice I overheard when I walked into the office. He's a short man, no more than five feet eight, but his bulky upper body and stout frame still seem impressive in an olive green business suit. His mouth twists into a crooked smile as he rubs his bald head. His medium brown skin reflects the fluorescent lights.

"It's fine, Mrs. Ruby. I will see her now."

I smirk slightly, feeling like I've won a prize. I say loudly, "Well, you never need to worry about hiring a security guard." Taking one last look at the old woman, she pays me no mind and resumes typing away on her computer, though she still eyes me ever so slightly.

"Hello, I'm Travis Spencer. I don't believe we've had the pleasure of meeting, and you are..." His hand extends to shake mine.

"I'm Maverick Robinson," I say, extending my hand as well. His strong grip catches me off guard.

We walk into his office, which seems more impressive than the sterile white lobby. A large desk with multiple degrees, professional accomplishments, and newspaper articles lines the back wall behind it.

A large area rug covers most of the hardwood floors, and a

small bar cart in the corner catches my attention. Making a mental note to look him up later, I glance at the small litigation award on the edge of his desk.

He motions for me to sit down in a small navy blue chair with a wooden railing. I rest my elbows and place my purse on the identical chair next to me.

"I want to be added to Miss Stone's visitation list," I say, vaguely.

He laughs at my vagueness. "Well, you'll have to be a lot more specific than that. Over half the reporters in the District of Maryland want to visit Miss Stone; double that if I include any crazy right-wing patriots. I don't believe Violetta ever mentioned having any sisters."

"That's right. I'm not her sister. Honestly, I can't even say I'm her friend. But I am someone who can help clear her name and help her get her freedom back."

His playful leisure quickly disappears, and his body language tenses, though he tries to hide it. He looks like a real lawyer now, measuring what information he can pull from me.

"And just how would you do that?"

"I can't tell you that. The only person who can decide whether she trusts you with this information is Violetta herself, which is exactly why I need to speak with her. All I want to do is help."

"Well, as you know, her time is precious ... there isn't much time before her trial starts. What guarantees can you make if I allow you visitation?"

"I can't ... but I can promise you she'll want to talk with me."

"I'm intrigued, but that's not enough. I'll speak with my client first and let you know. Leave your number with Ruby, and I'll be in touch within twenty-four hours."

"Thank you," we both say in unison. Mr. Spencer smiles

coyly ... before standing from his desk.

The playful charm returns as he steps toward the office door and opens it for me. He licks his lips slowly before saying, "It's been a pleasure, Maverick. If there's anything you need, let me know."

"OK," I say, uninterested in the way his eyes linger on me. But I know this is the only way to have an in with Violetta through her attorney, no matter how lust-filled his eyes are.

"The pleasure's mine." I plaster on a smile that says I'm excited and nervous and proceed out the door toward the exit.

* * *

I sip a double shot of brandy in the bar adjacent to the hotel lobby. My eyes wander to every person entering and exiting the doors, wondering who is watching me. I feel startled and paranoid from the bullet I found outside the hotel room, and I can't help but keep looking over my shoulder.

I've been impatiently waiting to hear back from Violetta's lawyer. It's been almost twenty-four hours, and still, no word from him. Flipping my phone over and over in my hands, I hope to hear something soon.

My mind drifts back to Jun Pyo and the things he did to this innocent woman. *But he didn't do the same to you. He protected me, my subconscious subtly reminds me.*

Not even wanting to go there mentally, I finish my brandy quickly to silence my thoughts. I flag down the bartender to get my bill. I can't be drunk right now. I need to stay focused and level-headed. As I wait for my bill and the bartender tends to other patrons, I hear someone behind me.

"Well, what an unexpected pleasure, Ms. Robinson. I thought that was you."

I swivel the bar stool around and see it's Mr. Spencer, the lawyer, dressed in a cream suit with a brown handkerchief. His bald head shines under the bar lights, and the air smells of a fresh, masculine scent from his cologne. He looks much more handsome than I remember.

"Hi, Mr. Spencer. How nice to see you. I guess this is a small city after all, for us to bump into one another this way."

"Please call me Travis."

"As long as you call me Maverick," I state quickly.

"Done... Yes, this city is somehow small enough to see a familiar face, but I'm happy I bumped into you. I was planning to have Ruby contact you tomorrow. I've agreed to let you visit Ms. Stone for now. There are some ground rules, but we'll discuss that tomorrow."

"Wow, this is great news. I don't have much time left before I head back home, and I'm grateful you agreed."

"This was not of my doing. Violetta decided for herself that she wanted to speak to the woman who had been so moved by her story and who could hold the key to her freedom."

"All right, I'll make sure to thank her."

"Of course... Well, I must be going, but it was good seeing you again." He licks his lips before rounding a corner and being escorted to a private section of the bar that houses a cigar lounge. With his exit, I finally pay my bill and head upstairs. Tomorrow it is.

* * *

The sound of my phone's alarm pings, indicating it's time to

62

get up at 7 a.m. exactly. I reach for the nightstand, silencing the noise, but remain wide awake. The lack of sleep I got last night seems trivial in the wake of finally meeting Violetta Stone. The night was one full of twists and turns, filled with dreams and questions about the man who had caused both my career and Violetta's to unravel. Even in all this mess, I still wondered what he was doing. But today, it was all about clearing Violetta's name.

An innocent Black woman in a country that wanted to teach her a lesson about treason, her case was all over the media. They had painted her as some super spy who was peddling government secrets to the highest bidder. Her case was being held at the Chesapeake County jail, which I would pass by on the way to the prison holding facility where she was being kept later that morning. Every local news station had an exposé on her life in the military, her career, and, more importantly, the delegates who had been killed, whom she was blamed for helping murder. Even in the wake of such a huge case, there was no explanation of why her case wouldn't be tried in military courts. Her case for being tried involved fraud from international wires received into her account that appeared to be payouts.

It seems like ages ago when I saw Violetta's file back in Seoul.

There were allies of American agendas, like the Green Coalition, that were about to expand their environmental act to an area in South Korea that had previously recorded dangerously high levels of corporate waste. The victim, Zhong Jhae, was supposed to sign the act into law, but after a mysterious drone appeared at the celebration, he and his aide were killed in front of hundreds.

Then there was the Ghanaian president-elect, Camille Addae, who was visiting Seoul on behalf of her country. She was on a path to become the first female president and held a strong stance against cobalt mining in her country, citing exploitative labor practices. But similarly, she was in a public space and was shot from a long range. There was never any confirmation as to whether the shot was fired remotely.

Although Chesapeake, Virginia, wasn't far from Washington, D.C., the capital's interest in the case was just as apparent. In multiple news outlets, there were requests for the case to be tried in the capital, but her lawyer had declared it unfit to move to a different jurisdiction, as I had seen in an interview. I felt sorry for her and wondered how having her life exposed and her freedom taken had affected her mentally. That could have been me, I think softly.

My mind races, thinking of all the things I want to ask Violetta and tell her as I lie stiffly in bed. But when I look at my phone again, I see the time is 7:20. It's time to get ready. Opening my suitcase, I look over what I packed, settling on a pair of gray slacks and a red V-neck blouse, paired with my black cardigan and flats.

Mr. Spencer sent a message later in the night asking if I'd like to ride with him to the Grand Mariner penitentiary. I get myself together, opting not to wear any jewelry, and have just enough time to swing by the Starbucks downstairs for a coffee and a bakery treat. As I step outside to wait in front of the hotel at exactly 8 a.m., I see a black SUV pull up, its impenetrable tint shielding me from looking inside. As the window rolls down, I see Mr. Spencer.

"Wonderful morning, Maverick. Let's go get our girl." His enthusiasm is contagious, and some of the knots in my stomach ease.

"Good morning, Mr. Spenc, I mean, Travis."

I place my coffee in the drink holder and take a bite of the strawberry Danish as we exit the hotel parking lot and head toward the highway. The car feels quiet, with jazz music playing softly. I hear the sound of the tires against the pavement, and Travis taps his finger lightly on the steering wheel.

"The drive to the prison is about an hour away, so please make yourself comfortable."

"Thanks," I say, not sure what to follow up with, but willing to make small talk. "So, how did you come to represent Violetta? Her case is something of a lawyer's worst nightmare, with how much evidence the media says is stacked up against her."

"Well, that's actually a funny story. I've been practicing criminal law for the last eight years, and of all the cases that get thrown my way, this is the biggest I've had. She was assigned a public defender who wanted her to contest her guilt, which, as you know, she wasn't willing to do. She wasn't about to give up without a fight. She asked her lawyer to get a phone book for the city of Chesapeake, told him to go to the legal section, and she landed on my name by chance. After that, she fired him and hired me. I remember thinking it must have been a joke ... but she was serious," he says, smiling widely, like a child on Christmas Day.

"Yes, that is interesting, but what made you take her case on? I mean, this isn't just a simple crime; this is serious business, going against the government and the military, and even institutions."

"To be honest, I'm not completely sure. I just knew this woman needed someone in her corner. I had to meet her first. In this business, sometimes it doesn't matter what you did, only whether someone can prove it. But I needed to look her in the eyes and know whether what she was being accused of was really something she was capable of. Sometimes the truth is staring straight back at you, and you just have to see it yourself." His eyes briefly land on me as he takes them off the road for a second. We lock eyes, and the smile from a few moments ago is replaced with a look of seriousness.

"I understand. Being in the military is the same in that sense. You're given orders and expected to follow them, whether you believe in the cause or not. But when you ask yourself if it's worth whatever you're being asked to do, a part of you has to agree so you can still look yourself in the mirror," I say, sipping more of my coffee.

The conversation continues easily as we both discuss our backgrounds and share a little more about Violetta. It isn't until we near exit 78, indicating the prison is up ahead, that I realize just how much time has passed.

"You know, for a lawyer, you're sure easy to talk to," I say as we turn off the highway and onto a busy intersection. We drive past a Walmart and a crowded shopping center where most of the traffic is headed.

"Well, I could say the same about you. Let's just hope my client feels the same."

I say nothing and instead continue examining my surroundings as we drive through the small town of Irvington, VA. The shopping center we pass seems to be the only sign of life, even as we pass much tinier homes that resemble slave shacks from the past. The fields of cotton seem reminiscent of another time and of a place far from where we are now.

As if he's reading my mind, Travis interrupts my thoughts.

"Irvington is a small town, there's not much here except that shopping area we passed and the prison that houses her.

Most people had no idea who Violetta Stone was for the first few months, but once the press made their presence known, there was not much left unknown. She became ostracized, and keeping a low profile became impossible. For the last six months, she's been in solitary confinement with limited interaction with anyone outside. But she's a fighter and somehow still has her sanity and her strong sense of innocence."

My heart sinks thinking about Violetta in a small, dark cell by herself, alone and innocent. I've got to make things right.

"If you don't mind my asking, maverick, why is it so important that you help Ms. Stone? You know she's never mentioned someone who could be helpful in the case, and to have you come out of thin air just seems almost too good to be true."

I stumble to find the right words as my tongue becomes tied, trying to figure out how to explain just how complicated my connection to Violetta is. Instead of spilling the beans and telling him every single detail, I opt for vagueness.

"I just know things that would help, and I believe in her innocence," I say curtly.

The truth is, I had been thinking the same thing ever since I made it my intention to try to save her. I don't know if it's because I felt guilty about Jun Pyo saving me but not her from a life in prison. I don't know if it's because it could've been me in her shoes. If I knew there was someone who could help, I would want them to.

Chapter 6: If These Walls Could Talk

The Grand Mariner prison looks like something out of a nightmare, with weathered barbed wire along the perimeter, tall brick guard towers, and overgrown grass. A welcome sign with faded letters and a lighthouse greets us as we pull up. Travis drives us past a large, overfilled parking lot with a few stray news anchors scattered throughout the lot. He navigates us to a more secluded area with assigned parking and pulls into a spot marked Personnel.

I hear the click of his seat belt unfastening, and he turns to me, looking to give what I presume will be a debrief.

"Have you ever been to prison before, I mean, visited?"

No, but it can't be much more than a woman like me has seen.

"I understand I didn't mean to be presumptuous. It's just that Mariner prison is different. Prisons aren't a great place to be anyway, but especially here. It can be a lot to digest if you're not familiar with it."

"I can handle myself," I say assuredly, not waiting any longer for him to exit the car. I pat myself down, making sure I don't have anything on me that's not allowed, like jewelry or my small pocketknife key chain, checking my reflection in the glass. Travis gets the hint and exits quickly as a reporter from sixty yards away notices him. We rush into the prison to avoid them, with little time to examine Mariner for myself.

Inside, a long hallway leads to a check-in area. Travis, already familiar with the process, leads the way. I follow, feeling an unnerving stench under my nose, a combination of fish, sanitizer, waste, and stale cigarettes. The floor looks dull, as if someone tried to make it look clean, but instead, a layer of dirt shines through.

We stop at the first post, where an older woman in a blue and white uniform has each of us fill out a guest form explaining our visit. Our pictures are taken quickly, like we're at a DMV, and printed out. The guard instructs us to place the badge on our clothing, then buzzes open a door into a second hallway leading to a checkpoint.

The hallways are quiet, but even with the thick concrete walls, I can hear sounds echoing as gates shut and doors close. Hurled curses, screams, and excited chatter, it's like being at a parade with all the different noises, leaving me overstimulated. We finally reach a waiting area that tries to appear normal, with a small corner of toys for children and a few old, worn magazines on a table. But on the far wall, behind a large male guard, there are multiple warning signs indicating that sneaking in prohibited materials is punishable by law. I can't help but feel uneasy reading all the warnings.

Travis speaks to another guard, explaining that we're here to see Violetta. This guard seems friendlier and offers a smile and a light joke as he directs us to a holding room reserved for attorneys to speak with their clients. Up until now, I've kept my mouth shut, simply taking it all in. The room doesn't offer much, just sterile metal chairs on one side of the table and one on the other, where Violetta will sit.

"Let's take a seat. They say it'll be a while until we can speak with her; it's lunchtime for her," Travis says.

I sit down on the metal chair and twirl my thumbs around each other as nervousness sets in. I should have rehearsed what I wanted to say; maybe then I would've believed the conversation would be easier. But there is nothing easy about this conversation. How do I explain that the man I slept with saved me, but framed her for crimes she never committed? How do I explain that I still have a flicker of hope in my heart for a man who could do something so wrong?

My heartbeat quickens, and suddenly, there isn't enough saliva in my throat. I begin to heave, dry coughing and gasping for air. I can feel my face flushing from embarrassment and strain. Travis reaches over unexpectedly, grabbing my hands, catching me completely off guard.

"I know this is a big deal for you, but Maverick, I promise this will not be something you have to worry about. Violetta wants to meet you, and I know whatever you've been holding in, she's open to hearing what you have to say."

Finally steadying myself, I place my hands on the table and do something unusual and unlike me. Clasping my hands together like praying hands, I think silently, This will all work out.

I hear a guard yelling, "Inmate entering." Stunned, I look up, not knowing what to expect.

As I look at the woman I've been meant to meet since I found out her true story, I see one thing clearly: the fire in her eyes tells me she is not defeated. She walks in, dressed in a dark blue shirt, thick khaki pants, and slide flip flops. Even in prison attire, her hair is braided neatly, and a sense of class is still evident on her face. She smiles at Travis as the guard moves her cuffs to the table. Even in the harsh sight of her hands cuffed in front of her, she smiles.

"Hello, Travis. I see you've brought a friend... Hello, Maverick Robinson."

Feeling like a pebble is lodged in my throat, I hear a nasal hello spill out of my mouth.

Travis jumps into the conversation, going over a few brief updates about Violetta's case. I hear none of what he says and instead try to read Violetta's body language. It's difficult to read, as most of her responses to Travis seem measured, with little emotion. But as Travis finishes his review of her case, he turns to me and begins speaking more directly.

"And now the reason why we're all here... Maverick, you said you had some incriminating evidence that could help my client. Let's discuss these findings and see what we can do together to prove it in court."

"Okay," I say sheepishly. "I'm not sure what we can prove, but I can tell you what I know. Before I start, though, I want to say I'm deeply sorry this happened to you. I can't believe the lengths people will go to hide their secrets. I can't promise I'll be able to answer all the questions you both may have, but I'll try my best."

I start from the beginning, explaining how I was selected for Violetta's old position as a drone intelligence operator. I tell her how, for months, I tried to get to the bottom of the claim that she was a mole, and how certain people believed she didn't do what she was accused of. I mention the Lotus crime organization and explain how they had an inside man handling their dealings. I make sure to leave out Jun Pyo's name for now and tell her how even he was used as a pawn, acting out of fear that his family would be further harmed.

As I share this information, I see compassion on Violetta's face, compassion she knows all too well. Once these people get hold of you, there's no letting go. I continue recounting my failed attempt to expose the Lotus connection and how everything blew up in my face. Emotionally spent from telling the entire story, yet stronger than ever, I pause to gauge Violetta's thoughts.

She hasn't interrupted me not once, but I can tell she has questions. Her lawyer, Travis, is moving his pen across his legal pad at a rapid pace, taking notes.

"First off, thank you for trusting me with this," she says. "I've been in the dark for long enough, and knowing I'm not crazy is bringing me a sense of peace I've only dreamed of. But I'm still confused about how you believe you can prove all of this in court. If this organization is as difficult to expose as you've said, what makes you believe so strongly that we can get to them?"

I pause before responding, "I'm not sure I can do it, at least not alone. I have an inside man who can help, but I can't guarantee anything. The last time I trusted him, I got burned, but this time I know we can make a difference together," I say firmly.

Travis interjects with the same skepticism that Violetta has written all over his face. "Maverick, this is a bold claim. We would need some assurances if this is truly a pursuit you'll make on Violetta's behalf. Right now, we have a case where, if Violetta pleads guilty, they are willing to make certain assurances at a parole hearing once this media attention dies down. If we pursue this, that deal could be off the table."

Instead of answering Travis, I turn toward Violetta, leaning closer across the table. With my elbows pressing into the hard surface, I sit on my tiptoes. "Would you rather serve time for crimes you didn't commit, or get your freedom, reputation, and name restored?"

Looking between Travis and me, Violetta does her best to compose herself, but tears strain against her cheeks. A quiet sense of relief fills the room, and with each passing moment, I can tell she's seriously considering what I've said. Finally, after shaking off the silence, literally shaking her head back and forth as if clearing the clutter of emotions from her mind, she says, "I want to be proven innocent. And I want my life back, no, actually, I want a new life, one where my name is cleared."

I can tell Travis wasn't expecting this conversation to escalate so quickly. He shuffles the paperwork in front of him and then picks up his pen, moving it rapidly between his hands. He abruptly stops and stares in disbelief. I can't tell whether he admires Violetta's desire to prove her innocence or whether his frustration over her backing out of the deal is what shifts his thoughts.

"Maverick, can you give my client and me a moment alone? I want to speak with her privately."

I get out of my seat swiftly, knowing they need to discuss the gravity of what this change could mean. Standing outside the room, I tap my foot, lightly anxious to know what the final decision will be. Although I have no plan and no idea how I'm going to get through to Jun Pyo or the Lotus organization, I have to figure this out. It's only right that her name gets cleared.

As minutes pass like painfully slow hours, the hallway remains empty and surprisingly quiet. Not even a guard walks by, but the temporary peace does nothing to calm my nerves. The thoughts running through my head remind me that this was an idea, not a plan. I drove here with the notion that I could show up and figure things out, as I've done most of my life. But staring at the closed metal door, I realize I'm in over my head.

Maybe I should have thought this through more before coming. Still, the fire in my chest tells me there has been enough waiting. This is the moment.

I hear the door open slightly and see Travis's head peek out. "We're ready for you now."

Walking back into the room, I notice the atmosphere has changed, and somehow it has become even more serious. But how could it not? Violetta's life is on the line. She's lost everything: her freedom, her career, and more than anything, her integrity. The world sees her as a criminal who deserves a fate far worse than jail time for the crimes she's being accused of. If my life were on the line, I'd be ready to listen to just about anyone willing to help.

Violetta doesn't wait for me to sit down before saying, "I want to fight for my justice, and if there's anything you can do to prove my innocence, I want your help. I can't offer you anything in return, but whatever you're chasing by being here is bigger than me or what I lack. You have your own reasons for being here. I know you haven't told me everything, but I don't care. I know you're extending your hand, and I'm going to take it."

I nod, not acknowledging her comments about the hints of dishonesty seeping through my story and my motive for helping, and instead extend my hand to touch hers. "Let's do this."

The rest of the afternoon is filled with endless stories from Violetta, explaining different assignments in descriptive detail from her time in Seoul. It seems like Travis and his pen can't write fast enough to capture every single detail. It isn't until a guard knocks heavily on the door, letting us know that visiting time is up.

Travis and I gather ourselves and glance back at Violetta, whose glimmer of hope seems to diminish as she's escorted back to her cell. I think of her on the walk back to the car, knowing that while we're leaving, she's still stuck in hell behind bars.

After entering Travis's car, I click my seat belt and hear the familiar sound of my stomach grumbling. That reminds me to think about something other than Violetta.

"Shall we get an early dinner?" Travis asks sheepishly.

"That sounds like a plan."

Chapter 7: Postcard from Nobody

What started as a weekend visit to right a wrong that wasn't really mine to correct has turned into a week of living out of a hotel. My suitcase sits atop the hotel bed, filled with a mix of sweatpants, cardigans, and underwear. After getting out of the shower, I realize I'm down to my last set of panties and bra, and I may have a problem.

After multiple calls from my family, particularly my mother, I've put them at ease by telling them I'm working, which is half the truth. But staring down at my suitcase, I can tell this impulsive decision is about to cost me a trip to the nearby mall. It's been ages since I've bought myself anything, but after working all week with Travis on Violetta's case, now is as good a time as any for a treat.

My last pair of sweatpants and a cropped sweatshirt will have to do. I take a mental note of the remaining inventory in my bag and decide that, in addition to grabbing my panties and a bra, I'll also need to get some clothes that aren't sweatpants. Travis mentioned meeting with some lawyers who would be assisting with the case for an interview, so I'll need proper clothes for that.

As I near the hotel door, ready to head out, I hear my phone ringing. I've left it on the bed under piles of laundry waiting to be washed. Reaching under a pair of teal colored track pants, I grab my phone.

Text Message from Travis: Violetta's legal team is meeting for dinner tonight. You're welcome to join; if not, I understand. Dinner is at 8:00 p.m. at Ransom Steakhouse.

I smile at the message and think about attending the dinner. My trip to the mall has suddenly become much more relevant. Texting Travis back, I tell him I'll be there.

Heading back out the door, I get into the rental and drive to North Shore Mall, hoping some retail therapy will ease this nervousness.

North Shore Mall is a premier outlet with everything from regular department stores to luxury brands for the affluent. The outdoor area features gorgeous waterfalls and a row of elegant chain restaurants lining its entrance. I can't help but think about my time in Houston, visiting large shopping malls where you could spend hours. Back home in Charleston, shopping for clothes was different. You could find valuable, unique pieces at local boutiques and thrift shops things like handmade jewelry and accessories that had been around for generations. That was the norm. But being here reminds me of the life I had before I moved.

I once lived a life of minimal drama in Houston, a place where I could spoil myself with anything and everything I wanted. Walking into a store and spending like there was no tomorrow was my lifestyle.

But now, after almost four months without a job and with my savings continuing to dwindle, I know a retirement check for my service won't be enough in the long term unless I plan to live with my parents for the rest of my life. With all the mess I've been through these past couple of months, my mind hasn't been able to make long-term plans. Still, as I pass the windows of luxury stores, I realize it may be time to figure out what's next.

The chatter of excited voices from small children, teenagers, and adults fills the mall as I walk past Macy's and into the food court. I can hear babies crying and cooing with their parents. Unlike so many times when the sight of a parent and child sent a shock wave through me, I am surprisingly unfazed. Instead of resentment and coldness, I'm met with appreciation and hope that one day I'll know that feeling, the love that comes with that kind of relationship.

A loud noise erupts near a sushi stand, and I turn my head quickly. A group of teens has started dancing, gathering an audience as one of them places a small plastic container out for tips. Although most of the crowd seems unaware, a few patrons stop to admire them as they perform all kinds of impressive moves, like spinning on their heads. I can't place the song they're dancing to, but I bob my head along with the beat. I notice a smoothie shop not far from the group and decide to start my retail therapy with a sweet treat.

After two and a half hours, my hands are filled to the brim with shopping bags, including a few new bras and panties, a dress for this evening's dinner, and a few other items I didn't need, including a Pandora charm bracelet. I feel my wrists straining from carrying the bags and hurry to the car. I stuff everything into the trunk and glance at my smartwatch. It appears I don't have much time to get ready, so I get into the car quickly. But as I click my seat belt, I notice a small flyer attached to the windshield. I flip it over, expecting it to be an ad for a local business, but instead, it's another postcard.

I look around, scanning the parking lot, but nothing seems

out of the ordinary as people continue walking toward the mall entrance. My heart thumps loudly because I know this isn't just a coincidence. The postcard reads, "Though your time is short, thank you for your visit to the port." A black and white lighthouse is etched on the front, with a small wooden sign that reads, "Come Back Soon." There is no bullet, but the message feels eerie. I can't help but feel watched as I back out of the parking space. My paranoia doesn't fade as I drive back to the hotel, constantly checking my rearview mirror for a car tailing me. But all I find is more worry, with no confirmation.

With my mind in a fog, I make it to my hotel room without making eye contact with anyone. As my eyes adjust, I notice my laundry neatly piled on the bed and see a small note from the housekeeper. My head spins as I think about someone watching me, someone I don't know. I wish I could talk to Jun Pyo. I need to understand why I'm being followed and harassed. My life is already in enough shambles; there's nothing left they could take.

I hear my phone ringing under the pile of bags I've placed on the bed. It's a call from my dad, and I answer quickly, my paranoia still high.

"Hey, is everything okay, Dad?"

"Everything's fine, sweetie. I just wanted to hear your voice. You know, this trip has me thinking about how this new opportunity is going for you. Your mom and I miss having you home."

I smile, picturing him sitting in his man cave, where he usually takes his calls.

"I miss you all too. I have to see if this new opportunity will pan out. I'll be staying a bit longer than expected, and I'm not sure when I'll be back."

"Okay, babydoll. Well, keep us updated. You know, we worry about you being up there by yourself. There are all types of crazy people out there."

I understand, Daddy, more than you know, but I'm safe, and I think I'll have a breakthrough soon so that I can come back home.

"If you say so," he pauses, and I hear some ruffling of papers in the background.

"Oh, and by the way, you got one of those postcards. It didn't have a return address."

My ears perk up. I wonder who it's from, caught off guard but still maintaining my composure. "So what does it say?"

My father takes a moment. "It's a postcard from Paris. It looks like some kind of message: 'To light the city you must be near, the Eiffel Tower let it be your spear. To rekindle what is lost, you must rekindle the flame. Meet us here in Paris, the City of Light.'" He stops reading for a moment. "There's no return address, but it's signed with the initial 'J.' One of your friends from the military, you think?"

"Yeah, it probably is." I sound unsure, but I know in my heart who the sender is. My heart skips a beat. So... he is in Paris, I say quietly, but not quietly enough.

"He? So you do know who this mystery person is. Does 'he' have a name?" My father's switch from dad to investigator should be studied in the way he asks these questions. I want to lie to him, but then I ask myself why I should. I'm grown, and I don't have to hide who I am from him, of all people.

"His name is Jun Pyo, and he was a former officer I grew close to during my time in Seoul. But we haven't spoken since I left, so maybe he's just curious about how I'm doing."

"Sounds like more than just a friend for him to send romantic postcards. Hmm, you sure that's all you two were?"

Growing serious over the phone, I say, "Without a doubt, we weren't more than that. I told you he betrayed me; there was nothing else to give. Does the postcard say anything else?"

"No, but you know, I think you got another one just yesterday. Let me look at the mail pile. You know your mother doesn't care where she puts that stuff." I wait intentionally, determined not to get anxious. He doesn't hold power over my emotions in that way anymore.

"Oh, I found it. This one is from Paris, too, but it looks like there's a small news clipping attached. There's something here about a new task force in Europe being led by a woman, Bridgette Copenstein. Not sure what that has to do with the postcard. This is strange," my father says, clearly confused.

"What's strange, Dad?"

"It's just that your letters were postdated months ago, but for some reason, we're only now receiving them. I don't know why they were delayed. I'll have to talk to that postmaster..."

My father continues, but his voice fades as I think about what he's just said. The letters are old, which means he's been trying to reach me. My mail could have been intercepted. With a million thoughts racing through my mind, I end the call.

In a fog, I sit on the bed for several minutes, processing how my life has already been upended, yet the torment hasn't stopped. Feeling monitored, stalked, and personally violated wasn't enough for these people. They still want to control my life, but I will not stand for it. I need to reach Jun Pyo and expose this organization. I refuse to hide.

Chapter 8: Ransom

The ride to Ransom Steakhouse is short but scenic, and driving along the coast feels like I'm in Charleston all over again. The special connection I have with water, and how it calms me, is powerful. Even with the uneasiness from today's call with my father and the unexpected postcard, my eyes drift toward the water, releasing pent-up tension. It's a full moon tonight, and the waves in the distance reflect a gentle shine that brings me peace. The steakhouse isn't far from the Chesapeake River, and as I pull into the parking lot, I can't help but feel butterflies in my stomach.

The gravel parking lot crunches under the rental car's tires, and I'm glad I opted for low-heeled mules. The lot is filled with nice cars, and valet parking sits beside the gravel area. I can't help but notice that Travis's car is in the valet section, and I see him stepping out. The small-brimmed hat he's wearing makes him look like an old Southern gentleman. He looks mature and handsome even from a distance.

I grab a spot close to the entrance and make my way inside. My impression of the restaurant so far is one of pleasant surprise. With the gorgeous waterfront view and the aroma of wood-fired steak in the air, I anticipate a good meal. As I near the door, a gentleman I've seen at the law practice appears to be heading inside as well. Although I can't place his name, we exchange smiles as he opens the door for me.

The restaurant's interior is lined with deep purple velvet booths and large tables. A few dimly lit tables sit near the entrance, but the best seat in the house is on the back deck, offering a clear view of the water even from the front entrance. I tell the host that the other gentleman and I are with the Spencer party, and she escorts us outside to the patio.

Seeing more familiar faces, I choose a seat a little farther away, where strings of lights and candles brighten the night. Fresh roses sit at the center of the table, and even as the sun goes down, the warmth in the air keeps me at ease. After being seated, I order the restaurant's suggested wine for the evening, an aged red with caramel notes.

I stare down at the menu, distracting myself from my lack of social confidence tonight. I hold it close to my face, trying to avoid eye contact. I'm not sure why I care what these people think of me. They don't really know me.

The menu appeals to my senses as I read through the delicious options. I lick my lips, slowly savoring the thought of Parmesan-crusted chicken or a buttered-to-perfection steak. I bite my lip, imagining either dish paired with crispy Brussels sprouts and homemade mashed potatoes.

Just as I lower my menu, still biting my lip, I notice Travis has joined the table. He's close enough to see me and nods in my direction with a smile as he continues talking with Brad, our paralegal. As I scan the table, I notice another familiar face walking in, it's Ruby. She hustles in with her usual pompous confidence, looking like somebody's grandmother, the kind who keeps peppermints in her purse. But looks can be deceiving. She gives Travis a pat on the hand and walks toward the end of the table.

As if the timing couldn't be more perfect, my glass of wine arrives. I take a deep sip, letting it settle on my tongue before swallowing as Ruby takes a seat beside me. She took time to warm up to, but now we're at least cordial and somewhat close, often becoming confidants when something strange happens in the office.

"Well, you know I've got to be motivated if they can get me out of the office," Ruby says to no one in particular. That doesn't stop her, though, as she continues. "I just can't deny a good meal from Ransom. They've got the best lobster tail in the city, and that's saying something."

I decide to engage and see if she'll keep up her signature spice and sass that I've grown accustomed to.

"So, Ruby, it's a surprise to see you here tonight. I didn't see you as the group dinner type."

"Oh, I'll be whatever type I need to be for Ransom, and since it's a company dinner, I'm going to eat my heart out." For the first time, I see Ruby in all her delight and heartiness; she's just a woman who stands her ground. Travis shared with me that Ruby was a retired receptionist but had to rejoin the workforce when her daughter and son-in-law unexpectedly passed away in a car accident. Her grandson, Ermias, needed a caretaker, and she stepped up. Her quick wit and tongue made her memorable, reminding Travis of his own grandmother. He instantly fell for her snarky responses to others, but she treated him with the utmost respect. Even in the sunset, I could tell Ruby was finally letting her hair down. As I continued sipping on my wine, my eyes grew wide at the custom cocktail Ruby had delivered to her without even ordering.

"What is that drink? I don't recall seeing it on the menu."

"Oh, baby, you wouldn't know nothing 'bout this... It's the bee's knees, taking me back home."

"Where's home?"

"None other than Chicago. They don't make good cocktails today. Sometimes, you've got to go with what you know, baby."

Looking at Ruby strangely, I blink multiple times, trying to figure out just who I am sitting next to. Her demeanor in the office is uptight and no-nonsense, but the woman sitting by me tonight appears to be the complete opposite.

The conversation at the table quiets down as Travis stands, clinking together his wine glass and butter knife to get every-one's attention. I'm intrigued by the way his smile warms up the evening and seems inviting. But sensing my thoughts are becoming anything but professional, I shake my head, hoping this will clear my mind of improper thoughts. I level myself out, handling the glass of wine as if it were fine china, and I motion it to my lips.

"I want to thank you all for coming tonight, and more importantly, thank you for all the hard work you have dedicated to Violetta and this case. When I was chosen to represent Miss Stone, I was confident that this woman was innocent. But it would take a lot more than my feelings to cover such a high-profile case. Without this team's expertise and tireless effort, we wouldn't be here. Although Violetta's case is still under the court's process, we are on the verge of something big with recent discoveries and a key witness."

As he says the last word, he looks towards the end of the table, making direct contact with me. I feel my cheeks flush, and the intensity of his stare makes me shiver. "Keep it professional, Mav," I think to myself.

The speech continues as Travis discusses key team members

by name and mentions the community contributions the public has made. It seems that more coverage is framing Violetta as a woman who was in the wrong place at the wrong time, rather than as a national traitor against her country and a criminal. I can't figure out how this shift happened, but it's been pivotal to her case. The evidence Travis and other team members have been working on seems to be the breakthrough he needs to clear Violetta's name.

The evening is full of excitement as the dinner chatter continues after Travis finishes his speech. It appears my glass of wine has disappeared, and before I can even contemplate a refill, a waiter walks my way and starts pouring. Instead of continuing to savor the rich wine, I decide to wait until I at least get an appetizer and order my main course. A few more people have arrived whom I'm unfamiliar with, but that doesn't make much of a difference as I listen in.

I find myself in this familiar, awkward, but somewhat comfortable two-step where I can be alone in a crowded room. The chatter from the table becomes quiet as I get lost in my thoughts, and everything around me becomes static. I find myself still delighting in the music and the feeling of tonight, but loneliness catches me by surprise. What should be an exciting, momentous celebration has somehow become muted in my own thoughts. But just as I feel myself being reeled in, I feel a small tap on my shoulder. It's Travis.

"I couldn't help but notice you're the woman of the night, seemingly by yourself. I wanted to introduce you to some of the important people in the case."

I smile shyly as he catches me off guard. "Let's do that another time. I just want to enjoy this moment. But I appreciate you whipping out your cape to check on me."

Seeming a little deflated from my lack of social apprehension, Travis still smiles, as sly as any lawyer or man I've ever noticed. But his poker face is poised as he sits down next to Ruby. He gravitates to her even among all of these people.

"Well, since I can't get Maverick to join me... Ruby, what do you say about making some rounds at the other end of the table?"

I look towards Ruby, chuckling and halfway expecting her to curse him out for even asking such a question.

"Now, honey, I love you bunches, but I will be sitting right here. I came for the food, plus you know half these people can't stand me, and I can't stand them," she says loudly. I snicker just above a whisper at her tell it like it is attitude.

But Travis gives an all too familiar look between the two of us. "I guess I already knew the answer to that one. Maverick, enjoy your meal. Don't forget to stop by before the end of the night. I'd like to speak with you. Ladies... enjoy."

As we both watch him walk away, a sense of admiration is on both of our faces. I really enjoy the way Travis has stood flat-footed in getting the truth for Violetta. His confidence is attractive, and his loyalty is sexy. Figuring I'll try to fish for information, I take another sip of my wine and face Ruby.

"So, Ruby, I was asking Travis a few days ago if there were any local spots that are nice for a date or special occasions, you know, somewhere he would take his girlfriend. Do you have any spots you'd recommend? I want to go to at least one more nice restaurant before I leave town."

"Oh, baby, I wasn't born yesterday. Travis has no woman; he's too busy with his law practice. But women still find a way to throw themselves at him," she says with that charm only she can dish out.

I continue chuckling for the second time tonight and feel happy once our food arrives shortly after getting schooled by Ruby.

I devour my Parmesan-crusted chicken and Brussels sprouts, leaving just enough room for dessert, a molten lava cake with raspberries and cocoa powder on top. I haven't looked up from my plate since it arrived, but as I come up for air, I notice most people have the same facial expression as I do: a glow from the delicious meal we all just ate. I feel tempted to ask for another order to have in the hotel room, but I decide against it so I don't look greedy.

After another fifteen minutes of letting my food settle, I decide to walk to the edge of the patio and closer to the water. As I walk to the farthest point, I notice a small pier further away from the crowd with a few lights. I am close enough to hear the river's water with the gentle knock of something against the pier dock; the peacefulness feels like a lullaby instead of a simple noise. I close my eyes, imagining I'm somewhere else.

"I thought I'd find you out here." I don't even turn around; I know it's Travis based on the deep baritone of his voice. "I see you're still not social, even after a wonderful meal."

I laugh, amused by his normal banter that I've grown accustomed to. "Well, the meal was delicious, and I needed to walk off some of it... who says I wasn't coming back to be social?"

This time, he laughs, standing next to me, close enough that our arms are almost touching. "Is that right? That would be challenging, considering most of the party has already left."

This time, it's me who whips around. The mostly full table is now about half empty, and the only people remaining are the young interns ordering drinks from the bar outside.

"Wow, I didn't realize people from Virginia cleared out that quickly."

"Normally, they don't, but tomorrow will be an extra-long day for most of us, and for those with families, they never stay long." Travis turns around, leaning his body against the wooden railing. He's poised to ask me a question, but he's thinking.

"You can just ask me," I say, trying to take some of the pressure off of waiting for him to ask.

"Why is it that a woman as beautiful as you is spending every waking moment helping out a lady she doesn't know, and the man who represents her, like it's the last thing you'll do? Over the last two weeks, I've seen you do everything in your power to help. I guess you could say I'm surprised there's no one you have to run back to. I apologize if I'm being too forward, but I must ask."

I turn my body towards Travis so that we're close but still not touching. I don't think twice about being ready to lie and make up some story, but instead, a voice of wisdom erupts inside of me, and I prepare to tell my truth.

"Well, first of all, that took a lot of courage to ask me that, and normally I would tell you that your forwardness is a turnoff, but I actually wouldn't mind telling you the truth." I surprise myself with the intensity and ferocity in my tone. "I fell for the man responsible for helping the Lotus, and I realized quickly that he had the opportunity to leave me with a fate similar to Violetta's. I was disgraced in my profession and left with heartbreak that, yet again, I'd allowed someone into my heart who didn't deserve a key to it. I work day and night with you all because it could have easily been me in a jail cell. I'm telling you this not because I want sympathy, but because I've made peace."

I pause, breathing for a few moments before continuing.

"I believe this person wants to make things right for Violetta, too. But instead of just hoping and wishing I could do something, I decided to come here with no plan and no idea other than that if I were in her shoes, I would want someone like myself and a lawyer like you to fight for me."

Travis's eyes go wide as he processes my words. He doesn't even respond, but instead pulls a thick cigar out of his pants pocket and lights it on the pier. As the sky has turned midnight blue, the orange end of his cigar provides a dim light.

"Wow, remind me to never ask that question again... now you know you just gave me the short version... some details are missing."

"There are," I say coyly. "I'm telling you this not out of obligation as Violetta's lawyer, but as a friend I've come to know."

"I understand... back to this statement about you finding me attractive."

The awkward exchange feels relieved as I laugh at Travis's sly attempt to flirt, and somehow, nervousness is the last thing on my mind. But staring into the night, I sense a new feeling of hope to love, or at least care for, someone new.

Chapter 9: Old Ghosts

In the case of Violetta Stone, there has been a public outcry from organizations across the country requesting that her sentencing be held in federal court. Just one week ago, an anonymous broadcast appeared, featuring a figure claiming she was innocent and that this was instead a mass cover-up for a criminal organization. Most people believe this could be a ploy by her legal representation. It remains unclear who is behind the video, and as tensions grow, protests have erupted here in Virginia. While Miss Stone waits to hear her fate, WKTV will keep you informed. This is Regina Vargas with your local news.

The office at Spencer Law Practice is so quiet you could hear a pin drop on a cotton pillow. The small boardroom is filled with Violetta's legal team, as everyone's attention is drawn away from the television. The legal team has been in a frenzy ever since the cryptic video about Violetta was shared. Between protests, a viral social media outcry, and phones ringing nonstop, things have felt endless. And now, with the local government becoming overwhelmed, Violetta's case has created division. Among her biggest supporters are Black women and veterans. The opposition, however, includes multiple right-wing groups that claim she should be executed to the fullest degree of the law.

Looking down at my watch, I notice it's five p.m. I exit the boardroom quietly, unnoticed, and walk to the front desk to relieve Ruby, who has to pick up her grandson. Over the last two weeks, I have felt more like a legal intern than a key witness, answering phones and staying late to help. I take the seat behind Ruby's desk. A few weeks ago, I stood in front of this same area, unsure of what to expect. But now, I've grown comfortable.

"Thanks, Maverick, for covering. Remember, if someone calls to submit a lead for the case, send it directly to line three so the legal team can review it. Some of these folks call just to play on the phone, if you know what I mean. See you tomorrow."

I wave as she exits, heading out the back entrance. For the next few hours, I received a few prank calls from organizations claiming to be interested in supporting the opposing counsel. One disturbing call says women who look like Violetta don't deserve to live; that number is immediately blocked. While aimlessly scrolling on social media, I stumble upon a post discussing Violetta's case and claiming it's a government conspiracy. But you can't always believe what you see online.

Before I knew it, there were only ten minutes left in my shift. As I stand up to grab a glass of water, I notice most of the lights are now off, including those in the boardroom. The only visible lights are on in Travis's office, though it's hard to tell when he plans on leaving sometimes. I think he sleeps here and secretly has a full bathroom and closet he uses. I knock on his door lightly and wait for him to say, "Come in."

He looks focused, intensely staring down at a brief, but as he looks up at me, I can tell he's trying to fight a smile.

"Maverick, I wondered if I was the only one still here; it seems

I was wrong." His voice is thick and deep, and his office smells of teakwood.

"I, hmm... I wanted to make sure the phone lines were covered since Ruby is out."

"Oh yes, how could I forget? Well, thank you. I know answering phones wasn't part of your role as a key witness, but I can say I've grown accustomed to seeing your face behind that desk, even if it's brief."

I blush at his comment but try not to get distracted. "Well, I just admire how hard everyone is working and figured I would too. By the way, Ruby asked me to put out a few more of the briefing packets for tomorrow morning since she'll be late, but I wasn't sure where they were. Could you point me in the right direction?" I hope changing the conversation will keep things from turning awkward.

"Yes, but I think it's easier if I just show you. The storage closet we keep them in is set up a bit strangely. If you don't know where to look, it can be challenging to find what you need."

Before I can even attempt to protest, he's up and walking out of his office into a supply closet I didn't even know existed. I follow him closely, and as we walk in, the closet seems much larger than I expected. There are row after row of wire shelving with all kinds of materials stacked against them, and I could easily get lost.

"I think they're usually over here," Travis says, walking to the far left and scanning a wire shelf, looking for the briefs. After a few moments, he looks just as puzzled as I felt. I turn around to the shelf opposite him and start looking at random shelves, trying to be helpful. Looking at the stacked items, I see labels meant to help find what we need.

"There they are, legal briefs," I say out loud. The briefs are in a container a few inches above my head. Standing on my tiptoes, I try to reach the box but struggle as the edges of my fingers grasp it just out of reach.

"Here, let me help you with that," I hear Travis say before I realize he's behind me, his long arms reaching over mine to grab the container. Even though we're not touching, I feel myself being drawn to him. I'm not sure if he feels the same, but he quickly clears his throat and avoids eye contact.

"See, I knew you would need my help," he smirks, regaining his contagious charisma. "I'll be in my office for a bit. Do you mind staying another twenty minutes? I'm just about finished here, but just in case any late-night calls come in."

"I can do that," I say, noticing my quickness in agreeing to stay with a man I barely know.

"Great, but fair warning, anyone who works late with me has to let me buy them dessert. How does coffee and a slice of pie from Chart's Diner sound?"

"I'd say you've definitely got a deal." As Travis walks back to his office, my mouth salivates at the thought of a piece of pecan pie from Chart's, a nearby diner that I've grown to love. But I feel my mouth watering for something else; too something this craving can't satisfy with pie alone.

* * *

I sink my fork into the thick slice of pecan pie, anticipating its sweet richness, and add a bit of Cool Whip on top. I take a bite and moan silently, or at least I think I do. Looking up across the table, I see that Travis looks amused.

"Do you and the pie need a moment alone?" he asks, laughing

at his own joke.

"Don't make fun of me," I say, smiling. "It's not my fault. They must have some sort of secret ingredient in that pie its soooo good."

"I'm sorry, but the noise you just made when you took a bite was too funny not to mention. But I understand. When I first moved here and started coming to this diner, I couldn't get enough of the chili and cornbread. Somehow, it made me feel at home."

"Interesting. I thought you might have been born and raised in the area. So where's home for you?"

"Denver. I was born there, and up until opening the practice here in Virginia, I lived there most of my life with a few brief stints in California. I would have settled there, but... things didn't quite work out that way." He looks down, fiddling with the salt and pepper shakers, and I know there's more to the story.

"So what was her name?" I ask, assuming his gloom is connected to a woman, since it's the first time I've seen him speak about something with so little enthusiasm.

"That obvious, huh? Well, her name was Celeste, and she was my fiancée. I had just finished law school, and she was on her way to becoming a physician. On paper, we were good together, a power couple, as people used to call us. But as we got closer to walking down the aisle, she grew hesitant about getting married. Instead of telling me, she wrote me a letter, blocked me, and never looked back. Long story short, California wasn't the place for me anymore. Too many memories had been made with her there."

"Wow," I say, simply thinking of what to say next. I'm surprised he shared this much with me, and I eat the last bite of pie. My heart hurts for Travis. Men like him, hardworking, good, and decent, deserve the world, but instead, he was abandoned by the woman he loved.

"Well, I guess she didn't deserve you then. You know, I personally think she cleared the way for the right woman to step in. I know about betrayal, and it takes a lot to forgive, but it's worth it."

"I know what you mean. I've forgiven her and myself. The signs were there, but I didn't want to believe them. Still, that situation pushed me to where I am now, and honestly, I have no regrets."

"I understand what you mean. Its funny how all the wrong things in life still seem to push us toward what we actually need."

"Yeah, things always work themselves out," Travis says before filling his mouth with a warm slice of sweet potato pie and washing it down with a sip of coffee. As we sit in the booth, our conversation shifts from relationships to politics, economics, and even science. I learn that Travis was once a political science major who wanted to be a politician but decided against it because of strong moral objections. I also discovered his love for science as he shares his fascination with space and asteroids. As he pays the check, he mentions a special he's wanted to watch, narrated by a well-known actor.

We walk outside, and as Travis escorts me to my car, we allow the silence to settle between us. As we approach my vehicle, I turn around suddenly, catching Travis off guard, and he bumps into me. I let out a shy laugh of embarrassment.

"I'm sorry; I didn't mean to surprise you. I just wanted to thank you again for the pie and say goodnight."

"No, I apologize. I was following you a bit too closely, I guess.

It's been a long day for us both, I assume. But you're welcome. I appreciate your hard work. Let me at least get the door for you."

I grab the rental car keys from the back pocket of my jeans to unlock the door and wait for Travis to open it. Instead, he pauses for a moment.

"I just wanted to say thank you for listening to me talk about Celeste. It's not often I have someone to share those things with, but for some reason, you have a special way of unlocking people. Have a good night, Maverick."

He leans in and gives my hand a gentle kiss, then releases it.

Now I'm the shocked one. As he opens the door like a true gentleman and waits for me to start the car before walking away, I can't help but feel special. The spot on my hand where he kissed feels warm and sensitive to the touch. And for a few quiet moments, as I drive back to the hotel, I feel that warmth spreading into my heart. Who knew such an innocent act could awaken something in me?

* * *

It's three a.m. on a Thursday, and as I blink rapidly while lying on my back in the spacious hotel bed, my hair and neck sink into the soft pillows beneath me. Even with the down comforter and sheets, sleep refuses to come. My mind races, thinking of everything and nothing at all.

I think about the way Travis kissed my hand the night before and how I wish he had kissed me somewhere else. I think about Violetta's case her innocence and how things have taken a turn, leaving open the possibility that she might walk away with her life intact. I think about Jun Pyo, wondering where he is and what he's doing. I think about the Crimson Lotus and dream of the day their organization is exposed for all the skeletons hidden in its closet. And I think about myself, thoughts swirling about what comes next. Once Violetta's case is over, what will I do?

I turn onto my side, facing the window. The blinds are still open from earlier in the day, and I can see the outline of the hotel roof next door. At three a.m., my thoughts compete endlessly for space. Feeling too drowsy to untangle all of life's complexities, I turn over once more and close my eyes, hoping rest finally finds me.

* * *

I groggily open my eyes, surprised to see that I slept through my eight a.m. alarm and now have to rush to make it to the law office. There is an important meeting scheduled for nine a.m., and that doesn't give me much time to get ready. After showering and choosing a black and white striped maxi dress with tan mules, I put my hair in a ponytail and dash to the hotel parking garage.

Forty minutes later, as I walk into the law office, I see Ruby at the desk in her usual spot.

"Morning, Maverick. Guess someone got in late. Thank you for covering for me. Travis wants to see you in his office right now," she says quickly, before I can even ask any questions. In typical Ruby fashion, she's already off to her next task, the phone to her ear as she dials a number.

I set my things down in the spare break room cabinet and walk toward Travis's office, curious about what he wants to discuss. I hope it's not about last night.

After greeting Hannah, one of the lead attorneys on the case, I walk to Travis's office in the back of the building and find his door open. I can see him focused on something on his computer screen, and he hasn't noticed that I've walked in.

"Good morning. Ruby said you wanted to see me? I also wanted to apologize for missing this morning's briefing, if that's what this is about."

He smiles at me, but it doesn't reach his eyes, which immediately makes me uneasy. "No, it's nothing of the sort. I wanted to share some new information I obtained with you. Violetta mentioned she wanted you to know. I spoke with her this morning."

"Okay... do I need to sit down for this? What's going on?"

"Do you remember Darcelle Ramirez? Violetta mentioned that you two had crossed paths in Seoul. Is that true?"

"Yes, I remember her. She was one of the first people who indicated that Violetta was innocent. I met her the night of a gala event in which my driver was almost killed. I haven't heard from her since."

"Yes. She and Violetta were very close friends. Unfortunately, her identity has now been linked to the mysterious video about Violetta's case that was released. She was found murdered in Salvador, Brazil. I have a contact at the embassy there, and it's still unclear what happened. Violetta said it was important that we make the public aware that Darcelle was an advocate before anyone else."

My heart sinks at the thought of the beautiful woman in the green dress from the gala. She was painstakingly determined to prove her friend's innocence, and knowing she was part of the video release suddenly makes sense. For a moment, I forget that I'm even in the room with Travis as I process the news.

"Maverick, you know I'm here if you need anything. This was not the news I wanted to share. Violetta is taking it pretty hard, as she and Darcelle had been friends for years."

"I'm not sure what I need right now. I didn't know Darcelle personally, but knowing she was murdered makes me feel uneasy, confused, and suspicious. I mean, how does anyone know this wasn't the Lotus organization or something connected to Violetta's case?"

"I don't know," Travis says, equally perplexed. "I can't give you the answers, but I am going to try to find them. Look, maybe it's a good idea if you take the day for yourself instead of being here today."

"No, I want to be busy. Plus, I need to figure out more for the case and for myself, for my own peace of mind. I think it's time I stop feeling like I have to look over my shoulder. I need more answers."

"I understand... but how are you going to do that?"

"I'm not sure yet, but I will figure things out. I won't live my life in fear." Standing defiantly, I feel determination and strength pulsing through my veins as I exit his office.

Silently thinking to myself, I repeat the words over and over again.

I won't live my life in fear.

I won't live my life in fear.

Not for anyone.

III

Part Three

Chapter 10: Paris

A new sense of motivation takes over as I open my laptop in search of more information. The only link I have to Jun Pyo is the French policewoman. I intend to find her, but as I browse the web, my feeling of excitement quickly subsides. It feels like I've hit a dead end.

Now that I'm no longer allowed to use the military database, I've lost my ability to thoroughly snoop on people. I've been restricted to searching the open web and scouring social media for clues. My subject is Bridgette Copenstein, the woman from the news clipping. I'm not sure why Jun Pyo would mention her, but she must be important.

I search my web browser for at least an hour, and all I can find is the original article clipping about her role in a new task force targeting global crime. It's as if she doesn't exist outside of work, no social media pages, not even a LinkedIn profile. I've run out of options and decided to see if Travis or Ruby can help me further. I know they have access to some legal databases.

"Hey, Ruby," I say, walking in front of her desk and resting my elbows on the edge of the counter.

"Hey, lady, I suppose you have a question for me?" She crosses her arms tightly across her chest, but her expression remains playful.

"How do you know that?"

"I could tell fifteen minutes ago when I saw your brow furrowed over there, not to mention those loud sighs you kept letting out."

Smiling, I respond quickly to her wit, not offended by it. Now that I've known her longer than a few minutes, I'm used to it. "I need to look someone up for the case. I'm having trouble locating her on my own, but I wondered if the firm has access to some expanded databases I could use to help me track someone down."

"Oh, that's easy, baby. Get one of the paralegals to help you. I don't use that mess, but they do and can get you logged in. I believe Jason is in the office today; he should be able to help."

"Okay, thanks. I'll find him."

"Great. Hope you find what you're looking for."

"Me too."

My best guess for where Jason might be is the large conference room, where most people gather to work on Violetta's case. As I walk in, multiple people are busy chatting, looking through paper files, and steadily working. I spot Jason at the edge of the long boardroom table and notice he's just finishing up a call.

Patiently waiting nearby, I admire how everyone in the room plays their part and wonder where my own career will land. With an almost complete military contract, I don't plan to reenlist after my medical leave runs out. The next step could be a private investigator, maybe.

"Maverick, I noticed you were waiting for me. Thanks for letting me wrap up that call. What's going on?" Jason says his Southern Virginia accent is as strong as his presence.

"I need to do some research on a potential interested party in the case, but I've found very little information on the subject. I wanted to see if there were any legal databases I could scrub, instead of the ones the firm normally has access to."

"Oh, sure, we have an international law enforcement database. Let me get you logged in under an admin account, and we can look together. I can't give you direct access, but I can help out."

"Not a problem. I'm heading out for a quick lunch, but I should be back by 1 p.m."

"Okay, I'll have it set up then. Meet me in the small legal conference room when you get back."

After taking a much-needed break, I sit in my car, dipping my last few fries into my double Oreo and brownie milkshake. It's a few minutes to one, and I'm anxious to see what Jason and I can locate on Bridgette. Feeling consumed by the desire to see Jun Pyo just one last time, I'm surprised to hear a light knock on my window. It's Travis, and as I roll the window down slightly, we make small talk.

Our exchange is brief and awkward, but it's a pleasant and welcome distraction that pulls my thoughts away from Jun Pyo. I can tell my time is running short, and as I prepare to exit my vehicle, Travis opens my door, smiling. He's just so lovely sometimes, too friendly, I think. Or maybe I'm just paranoid. A man can be kind without wanting something in return.

As we enter the office together, I notice Ruby make an odd facial expression, though she doesn't say anything. I wave Travis goodbye and walk toward the small conference room, away from the noise of the main boardroom.

"Hi, Jason. Thanks for helping me with this. Is everything ready?"

"Yes, let's pull the database back up. You can grab a chair

next to me."

For the next thirty minutes, Jason and I review everything we can find about Bridgette Copenstein. Even with the database using limited information, it's far more than what I was able to uncover on my own. We learn that the special task force she's associated with operates under INTERPOL. She's been an officer for the past fifteen years and specializes in gathering intelligence on criminal organizations. The only logical conclusion I can draw is that Jun Pyo is feeding her information, or perhaps someone close to him is. Either way, she may be the only link I have for now.

After thanking Jason for his help, I decided to call one of the phone numbers listed for Bridgette's local office. The phone rings, but after one final tone, a voicemail in French plays in my ear. I glance at my watch and notice it's around 2 p.m. In France, it's already about 8 p.m. The police office is likely closed by now, so instead of calling again, I decide to try first thing tomorrow morning.

* * *

Another sleepless night stretches ahead of me as I toss and turn, anticipating the follow-up call. I don't know what I'm expecting to uncover, but I feel on edge about whatever I might find. My phone alarm blares, signaling that it's 8 a.m. and time to head to the firm for my final day of preparation before taking the stand in Violetta's case.

As I sit up and let the sunlight fill the room, resting my back against the headboard, my eyes feel heavy. It's as if my body suddenly realizes how much sleep it needed but somehow skipped that requirement until it was time to get out of bed.

I arrive at the law firm a little after nine, feeling a quiet sadness knowing my time here is coming to an end. Being here gave me purpose and helped restore my focus. Still, all good things must come to an end, so we can continue our journey toward what comes next.

After walking to the nearby diner for one last slice of pecan pie and a hot coffee, I enter the law practice and am greeted by Ruby with her signature wit, though she's extra sassy today.

Settling in, I pick up my cell phone and call the same phone number as yesterday, seeking one thing: Bridgette Copenstein.

I dial the number quickly, looking down at a piece of paper with it written on it, and wait silently as the phone rings. I'm almost tempted to hang up and call back as the dial continues ringing. But just as I pull my phone away from my ear, I hear a man with a French accent coming through.

Although I'm not an expert in French, I know enough to carry on a conversation. I introduce myself to the officer and explain that I'm looking for Agent Copenstein, as I have information I can only provide to her directly. The man I'm speaking with is an investigator and assures me that I'll get a call back soon. But for now, the waiting seems immeasurable while he checks to see if she is in the office. The line is quiet, and seconds feel like minutes. Tapping my pen on the desk in front of me, I try to remain positive but grow more discouraged with each passing moment.

"Um, Miss... she is not available right now and would like to know if you can leave a message."

Sure... tell her it's regarding the new task force she's joined, and I have some information for her on a man named Jun Pyo.

OK, one moment. The line goes silent again, and I pull my phone away from my ear to make sure the call didn't drop. But instead, I hear a click and a woman's voice on the line.

"Hello, this is Agent Copenstein. Who am I speaking with?"

"This is Maverick Robinson, a former military. I need some help..." I stumble on my words. I push the next sentence out of my mouth like a gate struggling to open: "I am looking for Jun Pyo. It's urgent."

"And what would make you think I know who or where this person is?"

"I know because he sent a message, and you are the only person I believe he can trust right now. That's how."

"If you're a former military, then you know I need to verify what you're saying. I can't just release sensitive information to you. What do you have to share?" she says, pressing for more than I've offered, which isn't much.

"Look, I just need to speak with him urgently. A woman's freedom and maybe even her life are at stake. Do whatever you need to do, but I need to know within twenty-four hours if you can help me or not." I feel like the old me, the one who gave orders without hesitation. "Text this number, 930 403 5025. I'll be waiting."

I don't even wait for her to respond and hang up the phone, avoiding any unnecessary questions and answers I probably don't have.

Now I wait.

* * *

My testimony at the courts was harder than I expected. Although my testimony was strong and made it crystal clear that Violetta's involvement seemed extremely staged based on the drone attacks, the opposing counsel did manage to trip me up.

Mentioning my own personnel file threw me for a loop. Things still seemed unclear about what the intended outcome would be. With a two-week briefing for the case due to an upcoming holiday, the trial has been suspended. But the feeling of doing more has me at the Richmond International Airport.

Sitting outside the airport, I stare down at my phone at an international text received late last night that says:

He will speak with you, but you must be on the next flight to Paris. I will contact you when ready.

10:59 p.m.

In the passenger seat of Travis's car, he is every bit the gentleman he was earlier at my hotel, complete with a slice of pie and a card from everyone on the team. With my rental car turned in last evening and my flight back to Charleston canceled at the last minute, I happily accepted his offer for a ride to the airport. But now, sitting there, looking between the two of us and the doors to the international entrance, I feel an awkwardness that's been building finally surface in the car.

"I want you to know that when you get back, you've got someone waiting on you. Please have a safe trip to Paris, be careful, and let's bring this win home for Violetta."

"For Violetta," I echo. My luggage is on the curb in front of the drop-off area. I grab the handle of my suitcase, ready to make the trek to the airport security line.

"Just one more thing," I hear Travis say. Grabbing my hands from the suitcase handle, he embraces me and then pulls away briefly, planting a kiss on my cheek. Surprising both of us, I give him a quick peck on the lips.

"See you soon," I say, waving and walking toward the airport entrance. I can tell from the unexpected look on his face and the way he still stands there, somehow frozen in time, that he wasn't expecting that. I'm not sure why I kissed him back, but I feel he could be the start of something safe, new, and reliable.

As I enter the airport near my airline, I take one last look out the window to see Travis still standing there as a security guard tries to wave him over to move his car. But his eyes stay locked on me through the glass.

* * *

A night out in Paris sounds like the perfect antidote to such a lackluster visit so far. Sometimes, when you're seeking the truth, it finds you instead of the other way around. That's how I feel now, like I'm out here searching for anything that helps make sense of why my life was suddenly blown apart.

With a glass of wine I bought from a Parisian shop not far from the hotel, I pour the rich red liquid into a glass near the floor-length mirror in the hall. I admire the way my black lace bra clings to my shoulder, while a plush white robe tied at the waist slips slightly off the other. The blowout shows the full length of my jet black hair reaching the top of my back. With one hand wrapped around the stem of my wine glass and the other holding a tube of mascara, I take a sip and place the glass down.

Stepping closer to the mirror, I drag the mascara across my lashes, lengthening them and giving my eyes a sultry look. Applying a small tube of MAC red lipstick, my look is complete with minimal makeup tonight. Sticking with black, I let my robe drop to my feet and sink into the plush carpet as I grab a sleek black dress. The exposed shoulder and loose at the hips cut flatter my natural shape, making me look classy but still sexy.

To complete my look, I slip into an old but favorite pair of silver heels with butterflies on the back heel strap. I don't usually splurge on fashion, but these shoes are one of the most expensive things in my wardrobe.

With my look complete, I glance once more in the mirror before grabbing a small clutch with my phone and wallet. The night is lively as the Eiffel Tower looms in the background, sparkling, and the city lights up. The doorman opens the exterior door for me as I exit the Hotel Chanvieve.

I walk toward a crowded area in front of a small bar, keeping a safe distance from others, and nestle my way inside. Seeking isolation in a crowded room, I spot an empty seat at the end of the bar. Taking in the scene, I realize the bar isn't as crowded as I first thought. A quaint painting hangs on the far wall to my right, and bottles of different spirits line the bar's backdrop.

To my surprise, the bartender is a light-skinned man with freckles and red hair. Handsomely unique, he flashes a smile before asking, "Qu'est ce que tu bois?"

Stunned into silence, I find it hard to respond in the bit of French I picked up from my time in the Force.

"No trouble, miss. What will you be drinking tonight?"

Smiling widely and liking his English accent as much as the French one, I say, "Surprise me."

Looking over the bar, I admire the way Pierre shakes the ice cubes and mixture to make my French 75. A white long-sleeve shirt doesn't hide his muscles well as his arm contracts beneath the fabric. He smiles at me, dipping the rim of my champagne glass into sugar and pouring what will be my fifth French 75 cocktail.

Throughout the last two hours of our conversation during his shift, I've learned that Pierre has lived in Paris his whole life and has a passion for fitness, which explains those toned arms. He works here at the bar and is also a personal fitness coach by day, hoping to one day own his own gym. Surprisingly, he's very down-to-earth and quickly learns that I won't be sharing many details about what I do or why I'm here. Nevertheless, our conversation remains engaging as I ask him questions about being a Black Parisian and his upbringing, which he's pleased to share. As I look around the bar once more, it's still lively, with people tucked into dark corners of the room, sipping various brandies and wines.

My attention is drawn back to the bar when I see Pierre tug at his black vest to unbutton it. His chest rises slightly as he slips the vest off, and suddenly I'm very...no, extremely distracted.

"Well, my time here is done for the night... if you're interested in seeing the real Paris beyond the tourist areas, I'd love to show you."

"Oh, really? I could dream of nothing better than getting out of here and letting you show me the city."

"Say no more. Let me grab my things, and we'll be on our way."

Great. I swallow the rest of my drink a little too eagerly and stand near the bar's entrance, excited to see more of the City of Lights. The temperature outside seems colder as I glance out the window, watching moisture form on the glass from the heat pulsing through the bar. Just as I start second-guessing whether I should return to the hotel, Pierre steps out smoothly with a small black backpack slung over his shoulders and says a few words to the bartender now behind the bar.

Our eyes meet as he approaches me, smiling. "Let me show you Paris."

After leaving the bar, we walk a few blocks and arrive at a small one-story flat, which I assume is Pierre's home. It's a quaint neighborhood, nothing like what I'm used to seeing in the States, rows of small homes nestled close to one another. Pierre invites me inside while he freshens up, but I choose to stay outside, sitting on a small wrought iron bench in front of his place.

I watch cars pass slowly, my eyes trying to take everything in, noticing how Paris feels so different from where I'm from. In what seems like only a few minutes, Pierre steps back outside, no longer in his uniform. Instead, he's wearing loose jeans, a white button-up shirt, and a black and silver leather jacket. He looks even more handsome out of his work clothes.

Feeling a bit presumptuous, I reach for his hand, and he leads the way toward more adventure.

Pierre must be an unofficial tour guide for the city because by the end of the night, he's shown me everything from late-night cafés and beautiful midnight gardens that light up the skyline to a spot near the most gorgeous fountains. An array of stone statues and greenery fills the night sky, and as we stand beneath the Eiffel Tower, I think about the romance of the city.

"You know, I see why people fall in love with Paris. You have a beautiful city."

"Yes, it's nothing like what people are used to seeing," he says, giving an all too knowing stare into my eyes that makes me want more. The whisper of the wind moves between us, and I step closer to Pierre, standing directly between his broad, square shoulders. My lips are so close to his face that I can feel his breath against my skin.

Just as I close my eyes and he leans in for a kiss, I feel something brush across my feet. Startled, I open my eyes quickly and see a small animal scurrying away, its tail disappearing into the darkness. Jumping out of his embrace, I scream, "Was that a rat?"

Pierre looks at me, first alarmed and then amused. "The beautiful place is how you say it... also filled with rats. Because we are near the tower and the water, there is plenty of food nearby."

"Well, I take my comment back about the beauty. I can't believe that just happened." I feel my face flush with embarrassment, and I'm sure Pierre can tell.

"It's nothing. It happens a lot. But may I suggest we take this somewhere private?"

I take another step back from him, leaning against a nearby rail. I place one foot on the bottom bar, letting the other dangle loosely as I think about what he's said and what I want to do. Do I want a meaningless night filled with pleasure but ending in emptiness? The answer is no. Even though the familiar craving still lingers, it doesn't feel right. I know this is the right choice.

"I actually think that's not such a great idea. I'm kind of here to see someone, and I'm not sure how it will go. But I've enjoyed your time. I couldn't have left without this experience tonight."

"I understand. If anything changes, feel free to swing by the bar. I'd love to see you again. Au revoir, chérie." He mockingly bows before taking my hand and kissing it. After one last lingering look, he turns and walks away, heading in the opposite direction.

Using my phone for directions, I walk back to my hotel, proud of my discipline and knowing I'm leaving with my dignity intact.

I've changed.

Chapter 11: Reunited

"Are you Maverick Robinson?"

"Who's asking?" I say, suspicious of the tall woman standing in front of me. Dressed in a heather gray pantsuit with a deep burgundy bob, she looks polished and deliberate. I look her up and down, waiting for an answer. Something about the way she glances over her shoulder makes me uneasy.

"I'm really not at liberty to say, but I need you to come with me now. It's urgent."

I squint in irritation, rubbing my temple. Suddenly, the small outdoor café seating feels too exposed. The pistachio Danish and black tea are no longer appealing as my stomach turns queasy.

"Miss, please, it's about Jun Pyo."

I pick up my purse and place a twenty-dollar bill on the table.

"And for the record," she adds with an edge of attitude, placing her hand on her hip, "you don't know if you can trust me, but if you want to see him again, you'll follow me."

"OK," I say, exhaling sharply. "I'll follow you."

I keep pace as she moves quickly on foot, leading me in the opposite direction from the café.

"Hey, slow down," I say. "I agreed to come with you, but you need to tell me where you're taking me."

"Somewhere safe," she replies, still walking briskly as she cuts through a group of teenagers on the sidewalk.

"No. I want a real answer, or I'm not coming. Enough of this covert spy stuff." I release all my pent-up frustration at once.

The woman whose name still escapes me spins around on her black flats, stopping short. "I am trying to help a friend, and right now you're making it damn hard. If you must know, I'm taking you to a safe house."

"And where exactly is that?" I ask evenly, still unwilling to move another step.

"Well, it wouldn't be safe if I shared the location, now would it?"

I lean back slightly, my heel digging into the pavement. "Who exactly are you talking to?"

"Look, we can argue later. We're almost at the safe house. Please," she says, her tone softening.

I shake my head but continue following her. After cutting through a few narrow alleyways, we come to a stop. Across the street stands a row of gray stone cottages lined neatly together. The street is unusually quiet, with only a few cars parked along the curb.

The woman crosses the street, and I follow. As we approach the second cottage from the left, a weathered wrought iron gate, stained with copper rust, surrounds the quaint home. Just as she opens the metal gate to enter the property, I notice movement at the front door.

A white curtain is drawn back and then closed again just enough for me to sense someone standing there, though I can't see their face. Whether it's women's intuition or the butterflies dancing in my stomach, I know it's him.

Instead of taking the main door, the lady leads me to a side entrance that opens into the backyard. From the outside, the house is not impressive, as I glance back at a beat-up garden shed and dead flowers lining a rotting flower box. But I don't care about the details; I know why I'm here. We cross the threshold into the cottage, which smells of musk. I stare at the small kitchen we've entered and notice a tea kettle sitting on the stove.

As I take off my heavy jacket and catch my breath from the fast walk it took to get here, I lose whatever breath I have left when Jun Pyo walks in. He looks stoic, tired, but most importantly, hopeful as his eyes take me in. The smell of his signature cologne somehow replaces the musky odor of the house, and even in this setting, the pair of black jeans and dark gray hoodie looks out of place on him. The way his eyes don't leave mine nearly makes me ask what the hell he's staring at. Just as I begin to speak, the mystery woman starts talking.

"Pyo, we've got your asset now. We need to talk. You said you had some incriminating information to share, and I need to know now." She spins around, pointing at the sparse-looking house. "This doesn't come cheap or free. It's time to spill."

For the first time since I've met him, he looks out of control as his eyes dart between the woman and me.

"Agent Copenstein, just give me a minute to speak privately with Maverick. We need to talk, then you'll get your information." He sounds humble, almost submissive. This isn't my Jun Pyo.

My mouth hangs open as I look at the woman before me. She looks completely different from the image I saw on my computer screen. The red hair makes her appear much younger, and her slim build gives her an athletic presence. I can't believe I didn't recognize her, and the fact that she came herself rather than sending another agent seems strange if she's the one in charge. It takes all my restraint to remain silent as I hear her speak again in the same matter-of-fact tone.

"Fine, but no more games," she says sharply before exiting the cottage through the side door, pulling out her phone and speaking angrily into it.

Before the door fully shuts, Jun Pyo closes the distance between us, his arms ready to wrap around me. But instead of welcoming him, I step back, my thighs bumping into the counter as my hands press against his chest, stopping the embrace.

He opens his mouth, ready to speak, but instead, I slide my hand up and cover his mouth, silencing him. Since I last saw him, he's been the one talking, sending letters, explaining himself, trying to justify everything. Now it's my turn.

"It's time I talk. Just give me a moment before you explain whatever the hell this is. For the last few months, I've mourned something that wasn't even real. I've cried myself to sleep because everything I worked hard for in my career disappeared in an instant. I've wondered how a postcard could make my heart skip a beat yet leave me feeling empty in the same breath. Most of all, I've thought about what I would do and say when I saw you again. Cursing you out seemed likely, having sex with you seemed likely, but seeing you like this was never part of my plan.

"I knew I would show up eventually when you asked, but I came for only one reason: to tell you that I want to move on with my life. At first, I wanted the truth about Violetta. Then I wanted the truth from you about who you were and why you... loved, I mean, betrayed me the way you did. All you could offer me in return was the one thing that made my body ache. I'm sorry that the weakest part of me is what you still have a hold on, and not the stronger part of me. In the end, you've shown me exactly who you are, and I have to believe you."

After releasing everything I've been holding in, I place my hands behind me on the counter, steadying myself and using it for support. My heart feels lighter, and the truth of my words hangs in the air between us. Jun Pyo stares at me, looking more broken than I've ever seen him. But the spark in his eyes still can't be hidden. I know he's still glad to see me.

"A lot of what you said is right. You asked me for the truth, and I chose to be dishonest. I thought I was protecting you and myself, doing the right thing, but I couldn't have been more wrong. There's no way I could ever expect you to trust me again. I couldn't blame you. All I can do is be the man I should've been and make things right. I respect what you've said and want to tell you more about what really occurred in Seoul, but only if that's what you want. It won't be about us, just the details about Violetta and the people I was working for."

I look into his eyes and not his mouth, like I usually do, trying to keep my concentration. I do want the truth, but at what cost?

"OK, but only business, nothing personal. After all this, I deserve to know the truth. I need hard facts on ledgers or anything showing that the payments made to Violetta were forged. This is what I came for."

I can help with that. We just have to figure out a way to get the information over. So does this mean you'll work with me? Jun Pyo extends his body with his arms wide open.

Instead of leaning into a hug, I extend my hand to shake his. He looks down at my left hand, extended, and I hastily lift my right hand, remembering the Korean tradition. Even with my correct hand extended, he seems anxious for closer physical contact, but this is as close as he's getting. As we shake hands, a spark I thought had died violently flares back to life, a charged moment in the air as our palms touch and electricity passes between us.

The safe house we've arrived at is quickly cleared of any trace of our presence, and Agent Copenstein prepares a car to take Jun Pyo to a temporary, undisclosed location for the foreseeable future. The information he has about his organization is enough to compromise his safety, and he now has to choose whether to stand tall or go into hiding. I'm not sure which option he's leaning toward, but the way Copenstein stares at him suggests she wants a decision and fast.

With little time for small talk, we leave the house and head toward a train station where I can say my final goodbye. Sitting next to Jun Pyo in this car in Paris feels unreal. I can tell he's nervous, and his hand rests on my thigh for comfort. I want to pull it away, but stop myself. He's all alone right now. No one else in the world knows he's sacrificing what little he has left.

We pass the café I was at earlier, and the car accelerates as we approach a crosswalk. It feels like we're driving too fast as we cross another intersection, barely missing a cyclist attempting to cross the street. Looking perplexed, I say nothing, only glancing at Jun Pyo. Something feels off.

Our eyes meet, and his face mirrors my concern. Agent Copenstein and the other agent driving the car are unusually quiet, trying too hard to make things seem normal. I notice a small nine millimeter gun near the cup holder. At the same time, a sudden bump from behind interrupts my unspoken thought about the weapon. A sapphire blue BMW slams into our rear bumper.

This should not be happening. "What's going on, Copenstein?" Jun Pyo asks, his voice edged with alarm.

"I don't know, but this car has been trailing us for at least two miles. We can't tell who it is, but we will protect you," she says, now reaching for the nine millimeter gun I noticed moments ago.

The car accelerates, blowing through a red light, and with a sharp turn, I'm thrown into Jun Pyo's lap from the impact, my head landing on his shoulder, my hands against his legs. I quickly pull back, trying to regain my balance. I settle upright again, gripping the door handle to steady myself. His eyes light up despite the danger, and I catch a glimpse of excitement flickering across his face.

Our driver whips the car around and speeds down a narrow street lined with food carts. A sharp left turn sends us onto cobblestone and rough terrain. I twist around and see that we're still being followed. The tension in the car thickens, but we don't slow down, nearly colliding with another vehicle as we reach regular pavement again and head toward a large bridge.

Agent Copenstein faces the back of the car, speaking to Jun Pyo. "Now we have to make you disappear. This wasn't supposed to get out to anyone that you were working with us. The agreement hasn't even been sanctioned yet."

"What do you mean by 'not sanctioned'?" I interrupt aggressively. "You have him sharing information that could get him killed, but you don't even have clearance?"

"Listen, I needed the details first before I could make a deal. My superior isn't going to make any promises without specific proof, and someone had to meet you before he would talk. So what did you expect?"

Jun Pyo blows out a sharp breath, and I can tell by the way his brows furrow that he's thinking.

Everyone's eyes remain fixed on the car behind us, which seems to be picking up speed, but the agent driving is not easily shaken as he takes another hard turn. As we approach a small one-way street near the water's edge, Jun Pyo notices a second car, the same model as the first.

"Look, we need to leave here fast. Someone knows I was about to become an informant, and we can't risk staying any longer," Jun Pyo says out loud, speaking more to the entire car than to Agent Copenstein.

He continues, "I think we need to split up. I need to get Maverick to safety. I can't do that without getting her out of here."

"No way, Pyo. We can't risk it. Plus, you're already under investigation by Interpol. There's no way other agencies won't be looking for you in Paris," Agent Copenstein says firmly.

"Neither can you risk getting caught in an unsanctioned deal where you've put me in danger," he replies, staring directly at her through the rear-view mirror. His face and tone make it clear he's not backing down.

With another hard hit from the rear, Agent Copenstein blinks, unable to maintain eye contact.

"Fine. Meet me at the rendezvous point in thirty-six hours. I'll text it to this phone." She quickly pulls a burner phone from her pants pocket and hands it to Jun Pyo.

He takes it without hesitation and nods. "OK. That gives me enough time."

"And Pyo don't get any bright ideas in those thirty-six hours. And if you suddenly forget this conversation, the Lotus won't be the only person you'll need to worry about watching your back for."

Jun Pyo doesn't respond, but I can tell he's irritated.

"Thirty-six hours. Now get us someplace safe."

* * *

The small town of Chantilly reminds me of my visit to Jun Pyo's home. The quiet stillness and the absence of city noise feel unfamiliar, almost unsettling. We walk into an inn with an entrance no wider than a bathroom stall, and an elderly innkeeper sits behind the desk.

A frail, older woman with a hunched back begins speaking French immediately. I hear Jun Pyo respond, surprising me with how fluently he speaks. Something else I never knew.

The woman reaches for a set of keys hanging in numbered slots along the wall. As their conversation continues, I glance back outside the office window, checking for any movement. I never thought that being on the run with my ex shit, he's not even that my ex-coworker would ever be part of my life. But this year has been full of surprises.

Jun Pyo tugs on my shoulder, getting my attention. "The room is this way after you." He points toward a dimly lit hallway that leads to the rooms. The hallway is made of stone, and the crevices are open windows to the night air. I can feel the crisp wind blowing through, and it puts me at ease.

Getting settled into the room is easy, since I didn't have time to go back to my hotel to get my things. Narrowly escaping whoever is after him seems to be a challenge he wasn't prepared for, either.

The room's interior features a small twin bed, a round corner coffee table, and a chair. The décor isn't much different from the outside, with a stone wall separating us from the next room and polyester bed sheets. The room isn't particularly cheerful, but it's somewhere safe to rest. Turning my eyes toward Jun Pyo, I try to make light of our current situation.

"If only I'd remembered to pack more," I say awkwardly, not sure what I'm hoping to convey.

But with a serious look, Jun Pyo doesn't pick up on my humor. He immediately takes off his T-shirt and hands it to me. I try not to stare, but his abs and chest seem more toned than I remember. Unconsciously biting my lip, I quickly recover.

"No, I was just trying to lighten the mood. It's fine. I'll sleep in the clothes I already have on if just for a night or two."

"No, take it," he says, his arm extended. "It's my fault you're even here. It's the least I can do... Besides, I remember you looked nice wearing my T-shirt."

A sense of nostalgia washes over me, the familiar heat, the memories of shared moments between us. But the flicker of hope disappears just as quickly.

We've been down this road before.

It hurts, but I do what needs to be done, opting to change in the bathroom. The large T-shirt falls just above my knee.

It feels like I'm trying to hide. I told myself not to get too emotionally involved. Not to get caught up in him in this version of him. But I'm not as strong as I thought. I try to pack away the intense emotions, the craving for instant comfort, and lips that seem to demand a kiss. I wipe my hands over my mouth, still tinted red from the lipstick I wore earlier.

I exit the bathroom to find the room pitch-black, except for a sliver of light coming through the window. Jun Pyo is lying in bed with his back to me. I hear quiet whimpers escape him. Unsure what to do, I try to climb into bed as quietly as possible, but the squeak of the springs gives me away.

I can't go back down this road with him again. He deserves

everything he's facing. The inner war between my mind and who I truly am rages as I consider how or if to comfort him.

I stare at his back, and in the thin line of light, I see it. Ink etched into his skin a reaper and an angel locked in battle. A picture of the constant struggle between good and evil within us all. The tattoo, even in the darkness, pulls at me, drawing me dangerously close again.

I roll onto my other side, so we're back to back. I squeeze my eyes shut, trying to quiet my thoughts, his soft whimpers, and most of all, my sadness. It isn't easy, but I keep my eyes closed and allow sleep to come, holding on to the belief that choosing restraint is the right thing to do.

Chapter 12: Payback

My body wakes early, slightly disoriented, and my eyes adjust to the room. There's weight on me as I try to lift my arm. I realize it's Jun Pyo, his weight resting on me, his arms draped over my shoulder in a strange position. I try moving slowly so as not to wake him completely, but after a few futile attempts, I realize he's too heavy. For just a moment, I study his face. It looks relaxed, content, and peaceful. I almost don't want to wake him. But my bladder tells me otherwise, so I tap his arm softly, waiting until his eyes flutter open before saying anything. He wakes and looks mortified that his arms are wrapped around me.

"I'm sorry... I didn't realize I had moved onto your side of the bed. Let me move over."

"It's honestly okay... but I have to get up. The bed isn't that big anyway."

He laughs lightly before rolling back onto his side of the bed. I get up, tugging down the shirt that now seems to be riding up my thighs, and hurry to the bathroom. Looking in the mirror, I look like a mess. Coming to Paris with my natural tresses was not on my bingo card, but there was no time for hair appointments. The blowout I got is still holding up; thanks to the cooler Paris weather, it almost feels like fall. Thankfully, I look halfway decent. I notice the complimentary toiletries and am grateful for the chance to freshen up.

After changing back into yesterday's clothes, I sit at the wooden coffee table near the door we entered through last night. My stomach growls loudly, and Jun Pyo turns toward me, still lying on the bed.

"I guess we should grab breakfast," he says, rising quickly and heading into the bathroom without waiting for my response. When he comes out, his shirtless body is on full display, and I momentarily lose myself counting his abs as he scans the room for something.

"Have you seen my shirt?" he asks, pulling back the covers to check the sheets.

"Oh, sorry. I put it on the rack in the bathroom."

"Thank you... I can't eat breakfast like this," he says, gesturing to himself. He turns, giving me a clear view of the tattoo I noticed the night before.

As he walks out of sight, I smirk at my own thoughts.

Who says you can't go to breakfast without a shirt? I'd have dinner on his abs if I could if I were interested in that kind of thing with him.

"So, what's the plan?" I ask, stuffing my mouth with light, airy crêpes from the small breakfast spot down the road from the motel. The sleepy town feels almost deserted, and the shop owner seemed genuinely pleased to see us. Jun Pyo orders hot tea but little else, while my appetite remains steady as I move on to a second crêpe, drizzled with a special honey sauce.

"Well, the short answer is that there is no plan. I needed enough time to get you somewhere safe before the Lotus finds out you're here in Paris. The plan is for you to get on a plane back to the States today." He delivers it bluntly, like a father who's made up his mind and doesn't want any argument.

But I'm far from his child. I swallow the last bite of my crêpe and prepare to defend myself.

"Listen, Jun Pyo, I came here because someone we both know needs our help. Violetta is facing serious charges back home because of what the Lotus organization made you do. I can't go back until I have concrete evidence that could prove her innocence. Besides, they were already watching me... or more accurately, they never stopped."

He places his hot tea on the table, and his face turns a deep shade of red. With his fists balled tightly, he says, "What do you mean they're still watching you?"

"Exactly what it sounds like. I went to Virginia to speak with Violetta. No one knew where I was going, not even my family, until I was already on my way. Turns out my welcome gift was a bullet and a postcard, greeting me to the city. I knew it wasn't you... But I knew it was probably them."

"Are you serious?" he asks sharply. "I explicitly told them to leave you alone. Was it not enough that they ruined any chance we had at something real, and now this?" His voice tightens. "I never should have trusted them. Even as a child, I learned people don't give without thinking about what they'll get in return. That's why I have to stop them. Even if I have to do it alone, they're not going to ruin anyone else's life." He defiantly lifts his tea and takes a bitter sip.

"So again, what's the plan? They need to know they aren't the only ones capable of getting payback."

"Payback?" Jun Pyo asks.

"It means they should know we aren't afraid and that we can make their lives just as difficult."

He exhales slowly. "Then yes, we can do that. But are you

sure this is what you want?"

"I'm positive," I say flatly.

* * *

There isn't much time. I want you right now. Please," I whisper, biting my lip so hard I think it might bleed.

"I want this... I want you."

"Are you sure?" Jun Pyo asks quietly. "I wouldn't blame you if you were ashamed of me... of all of this."

"I would never be ashamed of you. This is what I've been fighting ever since I saw you again. I tried to resist it, but my heart doesn't play fair."

"But I"

"Stop. No more talking," I say, pressing my lips to his with urgency. I feel the heat between us flare instantly as he responds, pulling me closer. My arms slide around his shoulders as they belong there, my fingers tracing the edge of his new tattoo. My body trembles as his lips brush my neck, and I bite my lip again, trying to stay quiet.

"Maverick... you taste good. I've missed this," he murmurs.

"Maverick... Maverick," he repeats, my name falling from his lips.

"Yes," I whisper, barely audible.

"Maverick."

A gentle tap on my shoulder pulls me away.

"Maverick, you were talking in your sleep. Are you okay?"

"Hmm... oh." I blink, disoriented. "I didn't realize I had dozed off." Wiping drool from the corner of my mouth, I try to steady myself and sit up. Instead, I have to lie back down as a migraine begins to throb, the light streaming through the window suddenly too much.

I feel like my guilt is written all over my face. Wanting to escape it, I make a quick excuse and step out, heading to a nearby drugstore. I pick up medication for my migraine and a few essentials we didn't have time to pack: toothbrushes, deodorant, and two large bottles of water. Feeling a little like a tourist, I also grab an "I Love Paris" sweatshirt and a pair of sweatpants to change into.

I'm gone for about thirty minutes. By the time I return, my migraine has eased just enough for me to function.

As I knock on the door, not bothering to try to reach for my key while balancing the bags in my hands, it doesn't take long for Jun Pyo to open the door and quickly grab the bags from me. I walk in, plopping down on the bed like it's the softest, most comfortable thing I've ever felt. Although the walk to the drugstore wasn't far, the pressure of my migraine has intensified again. I lay on my back as Jun Pyo stands off to the side, placing the bags on the coffee table near the window. He seems unsure of what to say next, but I know if we really want to work together, we have to move past these awkward feelings.

"So..." we both say at the same time, and with a simple laugh, I feel the atmosphere shift slightly.

"So I wanted to say there's a reason I came all this way. I wanted to see if, outside of dismantling the Lotus. In the States, Violetta, she's going on trial pretty soon, and I know we talked at the house about you helping her..." My voice trails off, unsure what else to say.

He stands there, looking at me squarely. I can't tell if he's upset at the mention of Violetta again or if he's contemplating something else. But after a few moments of silence, he responds.

"I've been trying to do that behind the scenes. I've struggled for a long time to live with the choices the Lotus forced me to make. But in that situation, I knew I had to make it right. So I did something... something that's the reason I'm being chased now. It's why it's unsafe for you to even be around me... to be this close to me." He says this while looking down faintly and running his hands through his thick hair.

Now fully sitting up on the bed with my back against the headboard, he has my complete attention.

"What do you mean you did something?"

"I... helped. There was a video released a few weeks ago that I."

"Wait, that was you? That video was the start of her case taking a turn. I can't believe it. How did you even do something like that?"

"I have connections... but more than that, I couldn't let you remember me that way, remember me as a coward, allowing someone else to take the blame. I had to help. Darcelle was part of the reason I was able to make that happen, but now she's gone. And in one way or another, the Lotus seems to be cleaning house because of this whole situation. I couldn't just let things stay the same after everything they've taken from me. My family is gone. My life has been tied to them for so long. I can't even say I've loved anyone seriously, because my life has been one endless pledge of loyalty after another."

Feeling stunned, I sit in silence, listening to him. The things taken from him are things he can never get back. I think about how painfully lonely it must be, realizing that the only family he's known was really using him. They treated him like a tool, something meant to protect them and show loyalty at all costs.

I think about how little freedom he's had to live a life that's truly his own, instead of feeling as though he owes everything to someone else. A life that means constantly looking over your shoulder, never knowing real peace or happiness.

I feel sad for him, and if these past few months are anything like what his entire life has been since he left his family, I can only imagine the torment he carries. Trained to be a soldier instead of being allowed to grow as a person.

The room feels still for a moment, until Jun Pyo continues speaking.

"I knew I had made a mistake when I left your apartment that day, but I thought I could control things. I've managed to keep things in balance so many times before, but this time I couldn't just walk away. With them... they'll test you to see how far you'll go to prove your loyalty. I thought that if I proved myself, that would be enough. And now," he says, leaning down, wiping his forehead and pushing his hair back, "now I've got nothing and no one..." He trails off, not finishing his sentence.

My resolve to keep things professional and straightforward, and to maintain that fine line in the sand between us, begins to dissolve after seeing him in such distress. I get off the bed and say nothing, moving toward him and wrapping my arms around him, hugging him as tightly as I can without squeezing the breath out of him. I feel him soften and wrap his arms around my lower back. I don't want to move his hands. I don't want to tell him that his head, resting in the crevice of my neck, is not where it should be. But seeing him like this weakens me.

I envision him, with a nameless face, and his sister, Suni, as children not knowing what to do as immigrants, orphans in another country, seeing the Lotus as some kind of fairy tale godmother figure. My heart hurts for him. I don't care that I'm breaking my own rule to keep a safe distance from him. I don't care that his hands are on my lower back as he pulls me closer. It feels like I don't care about anything in this moment.

But as I hear my phone ping, I feel a jolt back to reality and pull away from him. Backing away quickly, I see it's a text from Travis.

Hope you landed safely. See you when you get back.

Feeling guilt for reasons I can't quite explain between a few nights ago and now, I struggle to understand what I'm feeling. A loyalty to men that technically means nothing to me, because I am no one's. I am not inclined to behave one way or the other because I belong to no one. Yet I think of the text from Travis, my reformed resolve not to sleep with the attractive bartender, and even now, standing here after consoling the man I once swore I'd never want to see again.

I feel uneasiness settle in, a fog clouding my ability to make clear decisions, and instead of pushing myself further, I opt for some fresh air and time alone.

I need a moment. Just going to get some fresh air," I say quickly and exit the motel room for the second time today.

Jun Pyo tries to stop me, but I'm too fast. I need a moment to decide if getting so close to the fold again is where I need to be.

I grab my coat and walk farther into the city, passing the drugstore I stopped at earlier. People's faces seem uneasy and unfriendly as I walk by, and I can't shake the feeling that I'm being watched. I stop at a nearby gate that sections off a cathedral with grand pillars lining the outside. Doors stretching at least twelve feet high feel daunting, yet inviting, as I notice one standing open.

Inside, there are rows and rows of pews, and it strikes me as strange that the entrance is so exposed. Still, I stand there for a while, trying to collect myself and my thoughts. The next steps I take need to be guided, not driven by anyone else's will. Although my feet begin to carry me back toward the motel room, I do my best to quiet my mind. The decision I'm about to make to seek revenge and team up with the person who betrayed me will be either the best or the worst choice I make today.

Chapter 13: One Night Only

It's been about five hours since I got back to the room, but it feels as though the space has been transformed into a command center, and my time to cool off has turned into a time of preparation for Jun Pyo. The bed is covered with all types of equipment, from drones to recording devices and stacks of information files. When I walked in the door, I suspected we would start figuring out a plan for taking down the Lotus organization, but it seems Jun Pyo was already a few steps ahead of me.

Where did all of this come from?

"I've got friends in low places," he says, smirking.

But I'm not amused. There are thousands of dollars worth of equipment lying on the bed, and those personnel files look confidential. My concern must be written all over my face.

"Look, Maverick, I'm impressed and grateful that you decided to stay and help me, and I do mean what I said: I will help Violetta. But this plan to get even with the Lotus has been in motion for a while now. Others like me want to be free from this organization. Our meeting just moved things along faster."

"But you told me there was no plan earlier. How did things change that quickly? If you want me to do this, I need the truth from you." I can tell I've hurt his feelings a little with my last statement, but I don't care. My trust issues and gut instincts seem to falter when I'm around him, so I need honesty now more than ever.

"I didn't want to tell you... I really didn't think you would stay with me after everything. I didn't want you to feel like you had to. I was going to help Violetta in my own way, one way or another, and help you too."

My eyebrows rise again, this time nearly to my hairline. "What do you mean, help me?"

"Exactly what I said. I know you've been followed. I've been receiving photos of you ever since you left Seoul."

"What... how could you know? How could they know?" I say, completely drained as I try to make sense of what he's telling me.

"I don't know," he says, equally confused, but his expression hardens with anger. "They sent me pictures to a postal box I still owned in Seoul. I stayed there for a while until recently. They sent photos of you in Charleston... even when you were" He stops himself.

"Even when what? What were you going to say?"

"Even in Virginia. They sent me photos of you visiting the prison where Violetta was, and a man... There was a man in the pictures they sent."

My throat tightens. I don't know whether I feel more embarrassed or more enraged that these people would invade my privacy in this way. Then there's the audacity of them sending the photos to Jun Pyo. A surge of anger rushes through me, and I can't contain the hatred I feel for people I've never met.

Jun Pyo continues, "I didn't want to tell you, but I thought you should know just how serious things have become. Ever since I abandoned my post, I've been a target, and it seems you became one too."

"Yeah, I did... I just think they've taken enough from me," I say, scrambling to express exactly what I mean. Wanting to switch topics, I ask more questions. "So what about your sister... what about Suni? Have you been able to contact her? Maybe she could help us?"

Jun Pyo's eyes drop to the floor, and his jaw hardens. He doesn't respond at first, but after a few moments of silence, he finally answers.

"Her help is not an option. She's made it clear even before this that her loyalty lies with the organization and not with me."

"Well, maybe we could try again."

"No. I said she's not going to help. Now just leave it at that," he states harshly.

I feel my nostrils flare at his words. I pushed him too far. I'm sure he's already considered who could help with the infiltration. The room grows tense and quiet. I want to call him out for his sharp reaction, but instead, I let the minutes pass until I hear him speak again.

"I'm sorry, Maverick... It's just that talking about Suni is hard for me. These people have brainwashed her so deeply that she won't even talk to me, let alone turn against them. She's very close to the leaders, and since they rescued us as children, her loyalty to them has been unwavering. She won't do it, there's no hope of her changing."

"I know, and I'm sorry for pushing. I just thought we could use all the help we can get. It's still not entirely clear what the plan is."

"Thank you for understanding. I think I can tell you the truth now about what needs to happen."

"Tell me," I say, picking up one of the drone boxes.

* * *

Meet me in the courtyard, the small note on the sticky paper reads. My heart skips a beat, unsure what this could mean. Placing the clothes I bought at the drugstore on the bed, I look simple as ever in the same outfit an I Love Paris shirt and sweatpants.

The courtyard has a few metal café tables and chairs, but one table is set with candles and food. The courtyard lights are on, and string lights hang from post to post, making it look more romantic than it probably should.

"I know it's not quite as fancy as our date at the stall, but I figured we could at least enjoy a meal together without feeling like either of us needs to look over our shoulders. I asked the innkeeper if we could use the courtyard, and she obliged, saying not many guests are here around this time of year. I just wanted to do something special."

I can tell he's nervous as his rambling continues. Feeling bold, I place my finger over his lips to silence him. "It's perfect. Thank you."

I can feel his smile beneath my fingertips as I look around, noticing the small vase of fresh flowers and breathing in the wonderful aroma coming from the takeout boxes arranged on the table. Jun Pyo pulls out my chair, and I sit down, still stunned by how something so simple could make me feel this cherished.

"This was really thoughtful... even with everything going on, you decided to do something special," I say, my smile now matching his.

"It's the least I could do. Maverick, I don't know what's going to happen tomorrow, but."

I interrupt him. "No, let's just think about tonight," I plead.

"Okay."

For the next two hours, it feels as though the rest of the world doesn't exist. Jun Pyo and I act like we're on a normal date, with no looming timelines or threats nearby. Even his phone has stopped ringing, I guess Agent Copenstein has given up on trying to reach him. We devour fried octopus and ravioli while enjoying a glass of red wine. Although we're out in the open courtyard, the intimacy of the meal and conversation makes me forget why I ever had rules in the first place about not getting close to him. The nagging sensation at the back of my mind quiets as I allow myself to be present in the moment.

After dinner, we walk around the small town, looking like tourists as we cover a near six block span of the city. The busyness of Paris seems to be nonexistent here. There are families with their children, pizza parlors, a neighborhood bar, a market, and a butcher shop that we pass along the way. We stop for a moment at a nearby open marketplace, where a few people are sitting, drinking, and talking. It feels like a night made for reminiscing as I think back to Jun Pyo and my first date.

As we walk back to the motel, someone on a scooter speeds past me, startling me. I lean closer to Jun Pyo, grabbing his hand out of surprise. I quickly stare into his eyes, trying to convince myself it meant nothing. Once the rider disappears, I keep my hand locked in his, unsure of what I'm doing but knowing it feels right. He glances at our interlocked hands, my smooth brown skin against his tan skin. He says nothing, but the way he tightens his grip and keeps walking makes it feel like no words need to be said.

We stop at a storefront pastry shop and split a chocolate croissant topped with pistachios. As we continue back to the motel, we exchange glances, both of us trying not to stare too long. The heat in my chest rises as we stop to toss the pastry wrapper into a nearby trash can. Jun Pyo reaches out and wipes the edge of my mouth, brushing away a stray smear of chocolate near my lips. His thumb is coated with it, and instead of wiping it on pants, he slowly licks it clean, never breaking eye contact. Feeling flustered, I step ahead of him, hoping I can quiet my urge to want him. But it only intensifies when I feel his hand wrap around mine again as he catches up in one long stride.

Once back in the room, I can still feel the intensity of him looking at me while licking his thumb clean. I feel my body responding to the possibility of one last time, one more moment of passion, one night of forgetting everything. It feels like a temptation I crave, the desire to be irresponsible for just one night.

I excuse myself and head to the bathroom, giving myself a silent pep talk in the mirror so Jun Pyo can't hear me.

I place both hands over my face, rubbing them slowly up and down, trying to make sense of these feelings rising to the surface.

You don't have to do this.

You made a choice; this is only business.

That dinner was sweet... and the way he was looking at me. Hmm.

I can do this. I don't have to sleep with him even if I want to.

I shake my head at my reflection, looking and feeling like a madwoman.

"Hey, are you okay in there?" I hear Jun Pyo call out.

"Yep, I'm good. Just coming out," I reply.

When I open the door, the room is completely dark except for a few candles placed around the space. All the equipment from earlier has been neatly stacked away in a corner. Jun Pyo stands near the window, his back to me, staring out into the distance. My body feels like a magnet, drawn to him, but I steady my nerves and hormones, sitting on the bed and keeping a safe distance.

Interrupting whatever thoughts he's lost in, I finally ask the question that's been sitting with me all night. "Why are you doing all of this, the romantic dinner, and now the candles in the room? I don't understand it. I'm enjoying it, but why now?"

He's still facing the window, but I hear him let out a breath before responding.

"I owe it to you. I honestly owe you way more than this, but it's all I can do within my power right now. I thought about you every day when you left. I couldn't stand the thought that the last thing you would remember of me was betrayal. I couldn't end things like that. You deserve someone who can give you all of their heart, not just a piece. Tonight is my moment to truly say I'm sorry."

He spins around as he apologizes, and now that we're face to face again, we hold each other's glare.

I look away uncomfortably, my heart beating loudly in my ears.

He inches closer and sits down on the opposite end of the bed. Getting closer seems like a bad idea, and I scoot back, my back pressed against the headboard, my head tilted away from him.

"Maverick," he says.

I love the way he says my name, the way the letters roll off his tongue, the way his accent slips a bit as he says it.

"Tomorrow could be the last time I ever see you again. I don't want to regret the last night I have with you. I know this isn't right, and I know I don't have the right to ask, but I need you."

My eyes open wide, and somehow the butterflies in my stomach expand as I imagine the kind of need he wants me to fulfill physically.

But something else raises inside me anger. An anger I've done my best to suppress ever since I saw his face again. Ever since I landed in this country.

"So you need me in what way? For sex for one night only?"

"You must think I'm crazy to agree to that after everything. You don't want me... me as a woman. Me as something more than just something to fill your moment of need."

"Is that really the excuse you have for trying to sleep with me?"

I say this now, fully berating him, not breaking eye contact. The nerve of him.

I know it's contradictory, but knowing that all I have to look forward to with him is one night of passion makes my stomach twist.

It's just like last time, my heart drops, and suddenly my emotions drown in a sea of confused doubt.

I close my eyes for a few seconds because I don't want my anger to blind me or make me unaware of what I'm actually saying.

When I open them again, he's sitting next to me, his eyes glassy with unshed tears.

He looks at me with a hunger I know he wants to express, but doesn't.

But I will not pull emotion out of him, not this time.

I think, pleading silently with myself to stay quiet, because

I've already said what I needed to say.

"I wish it could be more. I'll never know what we really could have been."

"Don't you understand that this doesn't end once we ambush them? They will always have a target on our backs."

"Do you know how it feels to watch the woman you love be harassed?"

"Do you know how weak it makes me feel that this candlelight dinner and cheap pastry are the best I can do for you?"

"I can't promise I can protect you. I can't promise that love will be enough. I can't promise a future or a family."

"My life will always be lived on the run, and if you choose me, yours would look the same."

"That's not a choice. Not a real one, at least."

He continues, now standing, pacing back and forth across the room.

"No one knows what it's like to feel betrayed by the very people who raised you, or to realize your real family is already gone."

"Do you know I've never even had a relationship before you?"

"It wasn't even real, but it's the closest thing to real I've ever known."

"Do you know what it's like to realize that even when you run, you're still not free?"

"Every part of my life since childhood has been controlled by the Lotus."

"And now that I'm finally standing up to them, it's too late. My sister's blind faith means she will never leave."

"And the one person I connected with, even if it was built on a lie, hates me."

"I know you do. A part of you will always hate me for what

I've done."

I don't interrupt, even though I want to, because he's telling the truth. I will always remember how he played me, and separating his betrayal from who he is will always be a struggle. I want to reach out to him, but something tells me there's more he has to say as he begins to pace faster. It feels like I've somehow become invisible in the room.

"I just... I don't know what's going to happen after tomorrow. I can't fathom putting you in even more danger. But I thought tonight would somehow be my last chance. I could be a ghost come tomorrow if things go wrong. I'm not going back into protective custody, I won't," he says simply.

Finding the courage to intervene, I quickly step in front of Jun Pyo, blocking his path and stopping him from pacing the length of the room. I can feel every ounce of nerves, worry, and disdain as I stare into his eyes.

I clear my throat and speak. "Listen, I'm sorry about everything. You didn't deserve to be abandoned and manipulated. Those people didn't care about you; they wanted a soldier." I grab his hands and place them in mine. "You realized it, and one day your sister will too. Just try to have faith. And as for me, I can take care of myself. All I need is your honesty." I surprise myself with the confidence behind my words.

Looking at his face, I see him exhale, his expression softening. He places his hands on my jaw and pulls me closer. We are forehead to forehead, and I don't pull away. I know he needs this if only for one night.

As he breathes into me and I into him, I open my mouth, and our lips meet. My thoughts go quiet, and a rush of feeling spreads through me. I feel breathless as he kisses me with urgency, lifting me off the ground. My legs move on instinct, familiar rather than foreign, as they wrap around him. My body aches for him.

I don't care about what I said I wouldn't do. I just want him. I'll figure out the rest tomorrow.

Chapter 14: The Backup plan

I hear the train whistle passing the small station not far from the motel we checked out of. We wait on the platform, anticipating a train that will take us back to Paris. We should be off somewhere, rekindling the same flames we did last night, but we can't. No, nothing in this life ever seems simple for the two of us. Instead of being laid up with my body wrapped around his, we are at platform six, waiting to ambush the Lotus.

I stare down at the suitcase Jun Pyo has standing next to our bench. The luggage is full of equipment, including drones, surveillance gear, and a gun. Jun Pyo didn't think I saw it, but I noticed it, along with all the other things that seemed to surface that day. I know it's needed, we're not exactly going up against honorary Boy Scouts. This is a criminal organization. I'm surprised there isn't more firepower or additional help involved. For now, it's a two-person operation, and I can't fathom how Jun Pyo's plan will work, but I know it has to.

Having become so wrapped up in his world, I realize I need to return to the Chanvieve Hotel to collect my belongings, but that feels insignificant compared to the danger we are about to step into. Even after three explanations and a full overview of the plan, I still have my doubts. But knowing Jun Pyo's expertise and trusting my own drone navigation skills, we have a chance.

The plan consists of a quiet ambush at a local Lotus hangout, a Korean restaurant nearby that operates as a front for the organization. It's located in the Belleview district, an Asian community in Paris filled with countless restaurants, shops, and markets. The place, known as "The Blue Spot," appears to be an ordinary Korean restaurant to the untrained eye, but beneath its exterior lies a vast network of tunnels connecting throughout the city, as Jun Pyo explains. Although the main leaders remain in Seoul, the Lotus has recently expanded its reach into other countries. They've found success trafficking in Paris due to its proximity to neighboring nations and its connection to other criminal organizations.

The Blue Spot is just one of many locations across Europe where the Lotus has been operating as a cover. The information Jun Pyo planned to share with INTERPOL included details about Lotus locations, bank account numbers, and trafficking methods. As part of his military responsibilities, he helped arrange safe passage for victims of North Korean false imprisonment. It feels unreal to believe he didn't know some of the people he helped could later have been trafficked into another country. But knowing his family's history, I can understand why he needed to believe that lie.

Our train finally arrives, and we board quickly, showing our tickets to the attendant at the cabin entrance. We choose seats far from the others so we can talk freely. The train feels far more luxurious than the Amtrak rides I remember back in the States. The seats are plush and comfortable, and the ceiling is glass, revealing the sky above as we settle near the end of the train.

I notice the way a few passengers stare at us is not friendly, not hostile, but curious. We stand out among the small number of travelers, most of whom seem familiar with one another as they move toward the opposite end of the train. A woman and two men snicker quietly, glancing back at us more than once.

I feel relieved when the door to the connecting cabin slides shut, leaving us alone. As the train pulls away, it doesn't ease forward gently; instead, it gains speed quickly. An introductory announcement plays over the loudspeaker, introducing the conductor and the estimated arrival time in Paris. It's an hour and a half away, including stops.

"So let's go through this one more time. I know there's no certainty this is going to work, but I need to talk about it again; it'll calm my nerves," I say, speaking to Jun Pyo, who's looking out the window as we speed past a wide field. I feel myself unconsciously bouncing my knee back and forth.

"Okay...we can talk about it again," he says, turning toward me and placing his hand on my knee to still the movement. "We'll be okay. I know them like the back of my hand."

"So we're aiming for a quiet ambush, one that makes it seem like we were never even there. I know that because it's a weekday, a drop will be made at the Blue Spot during delivery hours."

I listen attentively, waiting for Jun Pyo's detailed account of how everything is supposed to unfold.

* * *

On a nearby rooftop of an abandoned building between the Blue Spot and a sparse apartment building, Jun Pyo and I are nestled in between an old a/c unit chimney. There's a catwalk allowing us a perfect view of the comings and goings of the front door of the business.

The setup of drones with different surveillance materials is set up on the roof, ready to capture video of whatever goes down. The expected arrival of multiple Lotus members was expected to be at least an hour ago. Of the expected members present, the Lotus accounts and numbers guys that maintains transactions for the organization. But with a small window of time becoming closer, Jun Pyo and I have both grown anxious.

But just as Jun Pyo starts second-guessing if the intel he got was bad and starts trying to reach his internal contact, at least four large SUVs pull up at the entrance of the Blue Spot. A string of large-bodied men in dark suits and shades is seen exiting quickly. But in the last car are women, almost all of them are wearing worn clothes. All except one, she seems to usher the girls towards the building while the men look on. With a camera next to my drone remote, I replace the two and start taking pictures, distracted for a moment by Jun Pyo's voice.

"It's really her...eonni."

"Eonni?" I whisper, confused. "Your sister? What is Suni even doing here? You said she's normally in Seoul. I mean, what are the odds of her just happening to be here at the same time we are? This smells like a setup," I say, barely stopping to breathe as I guide the drone down nearby carefully and inconspicuously, avoiding unwanted attention.

He stumbles, and I can tell immediately this wasn't part of his plan to see her in the flesh. He averts his eyes as I try to read him, but I can't.

"She wasn't supposed to be here," he says softly. "Why would they do this to me?" He speaks as though I'm not even standing beside him on the rooftop. I can tell his thoughts have pulled him somewhere far away.

"Why don't we take a break? We've already gathered more

than enough footage and audio recordings. We still have plenty of time," I say, glancing down at my phone.

Jun Pyo doesn't respond. He keeps staring across the street at the entrance where his sister had stood just moments earlier.

His sister Suni was tall, nearly his height. Her long hair was a pale shade of platinum blonde, striking against Jun Pyo's dark tresses. The drone feed captured her sharp figure: long legs, knee-high boots, a mini skirt, and a jacket trimmed with a brown fur leather collar. The way the men greeted her made it clear she was respected. And even behind her sunglasses, I could sense that same intensity Jun Pyo carried.

"Let's stay up here on the rooftop. I don't want to lose any valuable time," Jun Pyo says, not waiting for my response. He walks to the opposite edge of the roof and begins that familiar pacing, staring down at the pavement as if it might offer answers.

I give him space and turn my attention back to the entrance of the Blue Spot, hoping we can still gather evidence against the Lotus. A few quiet minutes pass with little activity, but our decoy should arrive soon.

"Change of plans, Maverick. We need to engage them directly. I know this isn't what we agreed on, but I need to get down there," Jun Pyo says, walking back toward me.

His posture tells me there's no arguing with him, but going down there would be a suicide mission.

"Jun Pyo, this is a trap clear as day. You think it's a coincidence she's here today of all days?" I say, making air quotes with my fingers.

My words barely register. The wall he builds around himself feels impenetrable as his face hardens. I don't know whether my voice can crack the resolve set in his jaw, but I try anyway.

"Listen, they know somehow that we're here. That means this could be a setup meant to get you. You said it yourself: Suni won't break her loyalty to the Lotus. She's abandoned you before; what makes today any different? We have one job, and that's to clear Violetta's name by exposing the Lotus. Please," I say, my voice breaking, "I'm begging you. You can't go down there alone. I know you feel like a one-man army, but you're not invincible."

By the time I finish, I'm breathless. I stare into Jun Pyo's chestnut brown eyes, but the truth is written plainly on his face. He wants to get to Suni even if it costs him his life.

"Maverick," he says quietly, "my mind is made up. Everything you said is true. But if it were your sister down there... wouldn't you do everything in your power to try to save her?"

Now I'm the one pacing... I think about Shaunie, what if we shared a story like Jun Pyo and his sister? He's damn right, and I know there's nothing I can do or say to stop him. My mind races, searching for quick solutions so he doesn't get himself killed. With each step across the rooftop, my thoughts scan for a way to create a better diversion, one that draws people out instead of forcing Jun Pyo in. Then, suddenly, an idea comes to me. I stop in my tracks and face Jun Pyo directly again. I step close enough to be face-to-face, leaving just enough space between us to convey the seriousness of what I'm about to say.

"Listen, this is a suicide mission to go into an establishment that's full of gangsters and people who could want you and me dead," I say, pointing between us. "But you were right. If my sister were in that building and I knew I had one last shot at saving her or even seeing her, I would do something about it. To get her out, we need a diversion...a good one that minimizes the risk of you going in there and making it out."

"Okay," he says, nodding and waiting, holding on to my every word.

"The best we can do is get them to come outside. Now, I know you said there's a separate entrance people use that's a few blocks from here. What if we cause a diversion and force them to evacuate the building? That way, they'll be pushed outside, and Suni will have to exit as well. But we'll need to split up to cover both exit points, the front and the back. I can pilot the drone for surveillance once things get crazy."

"Maverick...baby, this is a good plan."

Baby, I think to myself, a mix of uncertainty and warmth passes over me. But with no time for pleasantries or butterflies, I continue speaking.

"The only question is what the diversion is? We could start a fire, or maybe trigger an alarm and hack into the electrical system, but that takes time. Or maybe"

Jun Pyo interrupts my rambling.

"I've got an idea. We have three drones," he says, walking to the suitcase and pulling the other two out. "So this one," he continues, picking up the gray Lear 3000 drone that I've used in the past, "can act as our electronic scrambler for any phones or communication nearby. I can set it up on autopilot. And this one" he lifts the Black Hawk, similar to the one I saw almost a year ago at the Gala "doesn't have any ammunition...But I think I can trick them into thinking it does. We swarm the building, and that's our way in."

"What do we do if this doesn't work? Is there a rendezvous point we can meet at that's not too far from here?" I ask, already thinking several steps ahead.

"The Love Lock Bridge isn't far from here. I noticed it on the way. It's a big tourist area, and we could easily lose anyone following us. Let's meet there," Jun Pyo says. Then he adds, "And Maverick...thank you. I know I'm asking you to risk it all again, but I promise this won't be in vain."

"I know..." I say dismissively, trying to push away the thought that things could turn left and leave me in danger. "Let's switch phones. I want to make sure I can remotely access the drone for coverage, since yours is already linked."

He pulls the burner phone out and hands it to me. I unlock access to the remote drone program and begin setting up the plan. The drone at the edge of the roof comes to life with a low hum. I'll have to turn off the signal scrambler, which means the phone can be tracked, which, for us, could be a bad thing. But knowing we have no other option right now, I turn off the scrambler app and look toward Jun Pyo, who is busy setting up the other devices.

"Jun Pyo," I say, and he pauses.

"I just want to say...I don't regret any of it. Anything that got both of us here. I hope after this, we can finally get a fair, honest chance. But I don't regret any of it..." My words trail as I struggle to say what's really on my heart. I hope he understands that I would rather be here with him right now, in this moment, than anywhere else.

He walks over, takes my hands, and kisses me on the forehead, then each cheek, and finally my lips slowly, deliberately, as if trying to hold on to every second of me. I can't help but think this feels like the last time...again.

"I hope so. I know what you're sacrificing by doing this, and it means the world to me. I hope I can repay the favor one day."

"Just meet me at the bridge, and that'll be a start," I say, grabbing him by his collar and nudging him closer to me. We kiss, and his lips feel like a dessert I can't stop indulging in the way his mouth covers mine, the heat between us strong enough to spark a fire even in a rainstorm. It takes everything in me to pull away, but putting our plan into action is what matters right now. The stakes are high.

After setting up the drone, I grab the phone from my pocket to remotely fly it for surveillance and give Jun Pyo a final hug, which he returns with a gentle kiss on my forehead. He walks toward a doorway leading off the rooftop and begins the diversion plan, setting a small fire near the back entrance of the Blue Spot. This should force everyone to exit through the front, but for those using the hidden exit, I'll be waiting.

After one final perimeter check, I leave the rooftop and descend a narrow set of stairs in the vacant building we've been occupying for the last two hours. I head toward the secret exit on Hopper St, just around the corner inside a local deli with an old butcher and a few customers. The marquee outside reads "Jelfand's Meats." I stand off to the side, still piloting the drone nearby.

The camera scans the entrance to the Blue Spot, and I notice people walking out in a calm but hurried manner. Then I feel a loud boom and see a small explosion on the drone feed, and I realize the fire has escalated into something that wasn't part of the plan. The next thing I see is people running from the front entrance. There must be at least twenty Asian women and men flooding out of the restaurant, but I don't see Jun Pyo, Suni, or any of the goons from earlier.

I glance back at the doors of the butcher shop everything still appears normal. But when I return my focus to the drone feed, I notice something else. People aren't just exiting the building. Another group has arrived. They're dressed in all black, wearing vests with large white letters INTERPOL. Within minutes, a fleet of vans, unmarked cars, and officers crowd the entire front entrance of the Blue Spot.

This is going left really fast. I look between the phone feed and the butcher shop, but there's still no sign of anyone. I know better than to stick around, especially this close to officers and agents swarming the area. I download all the drone footage to the phone and land the drone nearby, away from the chaos.

"I've got to get out of here. Jun Pyo will meet me at the bridge," I think silently to myself. Something feels off, and the queasiness in my stomach makes me feel like I could pass out. But I've got to go.

IV

Part Four

Chapter 15: All's Well That Ends Well

I'm walking swiftly now, following the GPS directions to Love Lock Bridge. I'm moving so fast that I can feel my breath shortening with each hurried step, putting more distance between me and the catastrophe I've left behind. I keep looking over my shoulder, expecting to be followed, but there's no one there. As I draw closer to the bridge, I see scattered groups of tourists on either side. Its railings are filled to the brim with locks of every color, and I move nearer, hoping to blend in while I try to pull up the drone feed again.

A woman accidentally bumps into me as I finally step onto the bridge platform, knocking the phone from my hand. It lands almost cinematically on the edge of the platform, and just as I reach for it, an unsuspecting child throws a tantrum right there on the bridge, his small feet and hands flailing against the wooden planks. His mother bends down to console him, but before I can grab the phone, he kicks it. It tumbles into the murky water below, and my heart sinks instantly.

What do I do now?

My small tragedy goes unnoticed as the mother scoops up her still wailing child, who writhes harder the tighter she tries to hold him. All I can see now is my hope sinking along with the phone, and I realize I'm truly in the dark with no connection to what's happening. I feel exposed standing on the bridge, waiting. Fifteen minutes pass. Then twenty. Then thirty. Still, there's no sign of Jun Pyo.

I walk the length of the bridge, pretending to admire the countless locks engraved with couples' initials. One catches my eye, a red lock with, ironically, the letters M + J. The universe, or maybe it's God, seems to have a painful sense of humor, taunting me like this. I can't wait much longer before I either go crazy or lose my grip entirely. The waiting is wearing me down, the not knowing slowly suffocating me.

A heavy feeling settles in the pit of my stomach, urging me to run. It's so strong that I feel my nerves shoot through my legs like electricity. Instead of second-guessing it, I listen. My inner warning bell rings loud and clear; something is about to happen. I step off the bridge, passing the spot where the phone fell, and head toward the nearby building with the bathrooms. I haven't left completely, still clinging to the hope that Jun Pyo might show up, but if someone is watching me, I need to stay visible.

I enter the women's restroom and slip into an empty stall, sitting down for a moment to think. The feeling of being unsafe settles deep in my bones, undeniable. Still, part of me wonders if I should wait a little longer to see if he arrives. Or if he'll leave me in the dark... alone...by myself, just like last time.

While pacing quietly inside the stall to calm my nerves, I hear a sudden commotion outside. Loud chatter and unfamiliar voices echo in the distance. I step out quickly and peek beyond the restroom entrance, where I have a clear view of the bridge. Armed guards now line it. I stare, trying to understand what they're searching for, when the realization hits me, they're here for Jun Pyo...or for me.

The bulletproof vests are unmistakable, each stamped with INTERPOL in large letters. There are about ten agents in total, scanning the area with purpose. I know without a doubt they're looking for someone.

The distance between the bathroom and the bridge is roughly a quarter mile. Most of the agents are clustered around the exact spot where my phone plunged into the water minutes earlier. That tells me everything I need to know. The phone had a tracker. It wasn't useful while the signal scrambler was on, but once it was turned off to operate the drone, it might as well have sent a message saying, come find me.

I continue watching from a distance and realize I can't wait any longer for Jun Pyo. If INTERPOL is here, Agent Copenstein can't be far behind. I leave the building and walk slowly in the opposite direction from the bridge. Tourists stand nearby, watching the agents' activity, giving me the chance to blend in.

The only place left to go is back to my hotel room to collect my things. I walk briskly to a nearby station, forcing myself to appear calm as I flag down the first available cab. Without looking back, I leave the area.

Being cautious, I've walked past my hotel at least three times before finally entering, careful to take four flights of stairs and check the hallway before stepping inside. The hall doesn't seem unusual, and I don't know why I'm so paranoid, but I step back into the stairwell, leaning over the railing and scanning both up and down. There's no one there.

Stepping back into the hall, I pull out my key card and hear the familiar buzz of the door as I enter. The room looks almost exactly how I left it, with a few clothes lying on the now freshly made bed. For the first time in a while, I feel like I can breathe. I take solace in the quiet of the room, glancing over at my luggage as I mentally calculate how long it would take to pack and catch a flight home.

But the relief is short-lived when I hear a knock at the door. "Room service," a faint man's voice calls out. I jump up quickly, not even glancing through the peephole, and start speaking before the door is fully open.

"You have the wrong."

I'm interrupted abruptly and stunned into silence.

Standing behind the hotel employee is Agent Copenstein. She's glaring at me, arms crossed tightly over her chest. She's dressed in khaki cargo pants, a navy jacket, and military-style combat boots planted firmly on the floor.

"Maverick Robinson," she says condescendingly. "We've been looking for you. You are the last person in contact with Jun Pyo, and we have reason to believe he will no longer be participating as an informant. Instead, he is now considered a person of interest in the cases he promised to provide Intel on. You will be detained, starting now."

As she speaks, a massive man with a red beard, mustache, and eyebrows steps into view behind her. His piercing green eyes send a chill through me as he moves forward, a pair of zip ties clenched in his hand.

For a brief moment, I feel paralyzed by fear. This is the most serious trouble I've ever been in. Not even my worst moments in the Air Force could have prepared me for this. I clear my throat, pushing down the rising panic, and force my voice to sound steady.

My body is framed in the doorway, the door itself the only thing separating me from Agent Copenstein, the red-haired man, and the hotel employee. I lean against the frame for support.

"I understand your concerns," I say evenly, "but what exactly would I be reprimanded for? I can speak with you freely here in my hotel room. I don't know where Jun Pyo is." That part is true. "We were supposed to meet one last time before I left. He planned to provide Intel after following up on a new lead."

Agent Copenstein's face flushes a deep shade of pink, and a vein running from her hairline to her right eyebrow pulses sharply.

"Maverick," she says slowly, "when I ask you questions, I expect the truth. The intel we have suggests you've been doing far more than what you're admitting. If you continue lying to me, you will be arrested indefinitely and thrown into a cell."

The glint in her eyes tells me she means every word. My mouth goes dry as I scramble for what to say next, but she doesn't wait for my response. She informs me that if I comply, the zip ties won't be necessary. The red-haired man grimaces, clearly disappointed at the thought.

"Let me just grab my things," I say, attempting to step back into the room and close the door.

"That won't be necessary," Agent Copenstein cuts in sharply. "We'll only be gone a few hours if you tell me the truth. Let's go."

I know I don't have a choice. I close the door behind me and cast a glare at the hotel employee, who smirks far too smugly for my liking, clearly pleased with his role as a decoy.

Downstairs, an unmarked SUV is parked directly outside the entrance. As I cross the polished marble floor, I catch the hotel staff watching me with quiet suspicion, as if they already know I've done something wrong. The sting of embarrassment rushes through me, and I lower my head, focused solely on reaching the vehicle.

Outside, the weather has shifted to gray skies overhead, a drizzle falling. As I'm escorted into the SUV by INTERPOL, only one thought echoes in my mind:

Where is Jun Pyo?

The ride to the INTERPOL offices is quiet, and we enter quickly through a garage at the back entrance. Once inside, I'm immediately escorted to an interview room that looks like it belongs on a crime show set. The room holds a steel table and an uncomfortable chair. Agent Copenstein and the red-haired man instruct me to sit, and then leave the room rather quickly.

I know I'm not being arrested, but being placed in an interrogation room still makes my palms sweat. Where is he? The breaths in my chest seem to compete for space, and when I tilt my head upward, all I can see is the harsh fluorescent light overhead. Help is not coming.

The quiet in the room is so complete that all I can hear is my own breathing. Each passing minute feels like an eternity. But I refuse to break. My military training taught me more than enough about the psychological tactics used to unsettle people. Instead of sitting tense and hunched over the table, I lean back in the chair, making myself comfortable, staying still because I know they're watching.

As time passes, my eyelids grow heavy, and I begin to doze off from sheer boredom. Just as my eyes flutter closed, the door opens.

"We appreciate your patience," the red-haired man says. "I'm Agent Greene, and you've already met Agent Copenstein," he adds, nodding in her direction.

"Now, we apologize for ambushing you at your hotel, but you're the last person known to have been seen with this man." Agent Greene slides a photograph across the table. It's Jun Pyo, wearing a thick jacket, his face clearly visible. "He promised us valuable intel in exchange for his cooperation. In return, he would've received immunity for crimes he admitted to. The problem is... he disappeared. After you left our colleague's supervision for what was supposed to be seventy-two hours, we lost contact with our asset. And now we need your help. Is there anything you can share with us?"

He stops speaking, and it's immediately clear he's playing good cop. Agent Copenstein, on the other hand, looks irritated and impatient. I weigh my words carefully. If I say too little, I risk suspicion. If I say too much, I could endanger both Jun Pyo and myself.

I keep my expression relaxed, a faint smirk forming as I sink further into the chair before responding.

"Well, for starters," I say calmly, "the way you embarrassed me at my hotel isn't exactly the best way to get someone to cooperate, especially when I'm a person of interest, not a suspect. I find it ironic that you felt the need to put on that entire show." I pause, then continue. "As for what you really want to know... I have no idea where Jun Pyo is. He's not with me. That's the truth."

I turn toward Agent Copenstein and meet her gaze directly. "Look, I understand he was supposed to return, but that has nothing to do with me. We discussed how he could help Violetta's case in the States and talked about moving forward from his past involvement with the Lotus. I wish I had more to give you, but once we returned to Paris, we parted ways."

Agent Copenstein stares at me as if I've grown a second head. The vein at her temple begins to pulse again, a clear sign she's ready to shift into bad-cop mode. I've said everything I intend to say. For the next few moments, I stare past them, silently praying this ordeal will end soon. Jun Pyo could be looking for me. I need to find him.

Her frustration finally erupts. Agent Copenstein slams her palm against the table, the sound echoing sharply through the room.

"Stop playing games with us," she snaps. "You were with him, and you have the tools necessary to help him disappear. We have CCTV footage of you. Do you really think we're idiots?"

My heart ignites at the words "footage" and "CCTV." The city's surveillance system is everywhere. She could be bluffing, or she could be telling the truth. Jun Pyo and I were careful to avoid obvious cameras, but there's no way to be certain. Instead of responding, I say nothing, refusing to incriminate myself further.

"Ms. Robinson," Agent Greene says gently, stepping back in. "We want to help you, but we need your cooperation. Jun Pyo is in serious trouble for evading authorities. He signed legal agreements to testify in exchange for avoiding jail time. Additionally, it's suspected that he was involved in a recent arson-related incident, which may have been an attempt to dismantle his former organization. Is there anything you can help us with?"

I blink but remain silent, staring through them as if they're made of glass. After several minutes, they both leave the room, shutting the door behind them.

My throat feels dry from shallow breaths and nerves. On the outside, I appear calm. Inside, my thoughts are racing, running a marathon at full speed.

No one knows I'm even here.

I don't have my phone.

What if they try to hold me overnight?

My passport is still in the hotel room.

They can't keep me overnight.

Where is Jun?

What do I tell them?

I don't know what to do.

After letting my brain run at the speed of an Olympic gold medalist, my thoughts slow down and eventually cease. A calmness sweeps over my body, assuring me that everything will be all right. I close my eyes again and this time allow the quietness to soothe me instead of worry me. Time in the interrogation room moves painfully slowly. I can't tell how much time has passed, but I guess that's part of the strategy to make me think about time. My thoughts replay the last few days and hours, going over every scene carefully. I chose to trust again, and it's landed me alone. Again. Still, I'm okay. I decided what my heart wanted: another chance to believe in love, a chance at revenge, and a chance to make things right for myself. This was all my choosing to help Jun Pyo believe that things would somehow work out. In the end, all's well that ends well, I guess. I'm in an interrogation room, and he's in the wind, drifting like daisy petals after a summer gust.

The room remains empty for what feels like two more hours before it opens again.

Agent Greene looks at me for a brief moment, then quickly starts rambling, "Miss Robinson... you are free to go. Thank you for answering our questions. Be careful for the rest of your stay. Please keep an eye out for Mr. Jun Pyo, as he's wanted as a person of interest. Here's my card in case you'd like to reach out. Enjoy the rest of your visit to Paris." He motions to the door, and I feel a wave of relief. But as I exit the interrogation room, I notice Agent Copenstein waiting near the door, and if looks could kill, I'd be six feet under. Her eyes cut through me like a serrated knife.

I exit the station quickly, not looking back, and find a nearby taxi to take me back to the hotel for now.

Chapter 16: One Last Time

The ride back to the hotel is lonely and cold. Rain taps steadily against the windows, and not even passing the Eiffel Tower can cheer me up. My mind is plagued by what will happen next with Violetta and Jun Pyo, but most of all by what I will do. I'm swimming in thoughts when I hear a phone ring in the back seat of the taxi. I try to hand it to the driver quickly, explaining that the phone is not mine, but he shook my hand away.

"Phone is for you, from a friend."

I look at him like he has three heads instead of one, then look at the phone in my hand like it's an unknown object. While the line still rings, I answer it quickly. "Who is this?"

"It's me," I hear the throaty, steady voice of Jun Pyo. My heart suddenly feels a little lighter, and my thoughts clearer.

"Where were you? I thought something bad happened to you. I thought you left me... I've been questioned, and I'm certain INTERPOL will be tracking me for however long I stay in the city." I try to speak in a low voice, unsure whether the driver is listening, but my anxiety seeps through anyway.

"I can explain everything. It wasn't safe for me. I... have something to show you, but only in person. Please meet me in... London."

"London? Are you serious, Jun? How am I supposed to do

that?"

"There's a train leaving in three hours. It's the last one for the evening, at seven o'clock, from the Gare du Nord station. If you can get there, I have a ticket arranged for you."

I mull the thought over in my head. If I could get what I came for, it would all be worth it. But even that thought makes me wonder if I'm lying to myself.

"OK, but I have to go to the hotel first. I'll be there."

"Thank you. This will give me a chance to explain everything, but be careful. I know Agent Copenstein is angry, and she'll use you to get back at me."

"You don't have to tell me that twice. If you could've seen the way she was looking at me during the interrogation, she looked like a dog waiting for a bone."

"I know, and I'm sorry I put you in harm's way again," he says. The line grows quiet, and I can tell his thoughts probably mirror my own from just moments ago.

"Miss, we are here," the taxi driver interrupts. We've pulled up to the hotel entrance. I get out quickly and try to pay for the ride, fumbling for my wallet, but I don't have one. It must still be in my room.

Before I can even apologize, the driver tells me my fare is already paid. "Bon soir," he says quickly, pulling off as soon as my hand leaves the door handle.

"Hello... hello, Maverick," I hear Jun Pyo say. I forgot the phone was still connected.

"I'm here. Let me speak to you when I'm on the train. I'll call you back," I say quickly and don't wait for him to say goodbye.

As I enter the hotel lobby, I notice a few staff members from earlier eyeing me. As I walk toward the elevators, a hotel clerk waves me over. Looking behind me and seeing no one else, I realize he's talking to me and walk closer.

Before he even starts talking, I try to interrupt. "I'm sorry about the commotion from earlier today."

"Yes, Madame. That is actually why I stopped you. We don't tolerate that type of behavior from our guests. I truly apologize, but we must ask you to leave. It's not a good image for us. I do hope you understand," he says curtly, and I can tell from the smirk at the corner of his mouth that he's expecting me to cause trouble. In the corner of my eye, I notice two security guards standing not too far behind me.

"No problem, sir. I'll just be grabbing my things," I say, attempting to walk away. But before I can even lift my feet, a bellhop appears with my luggage in hand, my purse and passport resting neatly on top.

"We have taken the liberty of packing all of your things. I can assure you these are all of your belongings."

My jaw drops in surprise. They packed my things to ensure I wouldn't return to the room. I'm in shock. "Wow, what a gesture. I would still like to make sure this is everything. Is there someone who can escort me back to the room to ensure none of my items are missing? I would hate to have to come back."

He breathes loudly, hesitates, then says, "Yes, Madame. Let me escort you up."

I glance at the phone and notice it's almost five p.m. "Let's hurry it up." He gives me a look but walks briskly toward the elevator.

The ride up is quiet. When the door opens, the room looks spotless, the bed made, a fresh towel folded into a swan placed neatly at the center. My pulse quickens as embarrassment washes over me. I walk to the bed and pull back the sheets.

The swan crumples to the floor, reduced to nothing more than a pile of towels.

"Have to make sure I didn't leave anything in the bed," I say to no one in particular. I walk into the restroom next, opening cabinets and pulling the curtain back to ensure nothing is left behind. But the room is bare. I stalk back into the main room, open the closet door, and see nothing.

"Thank you. I believe there is nothing of mine left." Without another word, we go downstairs, and I'm handed my belongings like a guest being thrown out for unruly behavior. I exit the hotel and hold my head high, trying to wave down another taxi so I can get to the train station on time.

* * *

The check-in counter at Gare du Nord station is long, with people buying last-minute tickets. The station offers routes to London, Brussels, Amsterdam, and nearby towns. I check the phone and see it's almost five thirty, tapping my feet impatiently as I count about ten people in front of me. Over the loudspeaker, I hear, "Train F1334 to London will end boarding in fifteen minutes." I close my eyes. I need a miracle to make it there in time.

My prayers are answered when another ticket booth opens, and the line begins to move faster. When it's finally my turn, I provide the attendant with my name and passport, explaining that a ticket has been left for me. After a few keystrokes, she locates it and prints a paper ticket.

"Madame, enjoy your ride to London. Next person, please."

And just like that, I'm on Train F1334. The train is nothing like anything I've seen before, vast and polished, with a large silver

Eurostar logo along the side. The conductor greets passengers as they board, and after I show my ticket, he points me toward my car.

I walk past multiple seats, balancing my luggage and purse in my hands. I enter a second car that feels more private and quieter, tucked away from the chatter of people, children, and families. The car is divided into small suites, and when I glance down at my ticket, I see Suite 6F marked.

I continue down the corridor and find the door to the private suite closed. Using the code printed on my ticket, I open the door and step inside. The space feels far too large for just me. There are two beds, a small table, and even a bathroom.

The lights are already on, but no one is here. I sit on a small couch by the window, looking out past the station toward a cluster of trees leading into the woods. I walk around the suite and notice a connecting door. When I place my hand on the handle, I can tell it's locked.

The suite is tastefully decorated in navy blue and gold, but none of it explains why I'm here. The ride from Paris to London is less than three hours. I wouldn't need all this space. Still puzzled, I sit down again and watch the scenery slide by as the train begins to move, creeping at first before picking up speed.

A faint knock at the door makes me wonder if I imagined it. Then I hear it again. I lean toward the peephole and press my left eye against it. I'm almost as angry as I am surprised.

It's Jun Pyo.

I open the slatted door quickly. He's standing there in the same clothes from earlier, though now they look worn and faded. I don't hesitate. I pull him inside, glancing up and down the corridor to make sure no one sees him or me.

"What are you doing here? You said we were meeting in

London... not riding the train together. This is too dangerous, too risky," I say, my mouth moving faster than I can even comprehend. But within seconds, I feel Jun Pyo's arms wrap around my waist. He inhales my scent and kisses me on the cheek.

"I'll explain, baby. Just let me savor this...I didn't think I'd see you again." Suddenly, I'm inhaling his scent too, getting so worked up that I forget the last time I saw him could have really been the last time. We stand there for a moment, and my nerves begin to melt, but my curiosity still lingers. I need answers.

"Let's sit down," he says, leading me back to the small couch by the train's window. We are now moving at full speed, trees rushing past as we leave a small town behind.

My hands rest comfortably in Jun Pyo's palms, and I feel warmth. "So what happened today?"

He clears his throat and looks deeply into my eyes before beginning. "I tried to use the drone as a distraction, but it wasn't working. I had to set a small fire near the entrance, not knowing there were flammable items nearby. The entire front entrance was set ablaze, and before I knew it, I couldn't contain it. I waited near the back entrance, but there were so many people running out."

"Did anybody get hurt?" I ask, not entirely sure I want to know the answer.

"I don't think so. I did manage to gather footage of some pretty influential men from the Lotus and can link them back to several trafficking crimes they're wanted for. But mostly, there were patrons."

"So what about Suni?" I ask quickly, cutting him off mid-sentence.

"I saw her, but there wasn't much time to talk, so I had to cause another diversion." His eyes drop to the floor, and he struggles to lift them again. I place my hands on his chin, gently lifting his face.

"What kind of diversion?"

"I had to fire my weapon...it was a flesh wound to someone near her. I didn't kill anyone, but it was the only way to separate her from them. Once I got to her, she started talking nonsense. She kept saying I was insane for going against family, asking me what had changed how one woman could make me turn against the Lotus...the people who raised us."

My eyes widen at his words because I know the woman he's talking about is me.

"You should have heard the things she was saying," he adds. From Jun Pyo's body language, it's clear he's frustrated.

"Well, we knew that would happen. She's been brainwashed by those people and that organization. Where is she now?"

Jun Pyo looks down again, like there's something he isn't telling me. I lift his head once more, this time forcing him to look me directly in the eyes.

"What else aren't you telling me?"

He stands abruptly and punches in a code, opening the connecting door I tried earlier. I follow him into the adjoining suite, which is set up identically to mine. The only difference is the woman lying on the bed. She appears unconscious. As I step closer, I recognize her immediately. It's Suni, still wearing the same clothes from earlier.

"Are you trying to tell me no, show me that you kidnapped your sister?"

"Well, technically, she's not a kid," he says quietly. "It's more like abducted."

Chapter 17: Truth Hurts

Are you trying to tell—-no show me that you kidnapped your sister?

Well, technically, she's not a kid... It's more like abducted.

I stare at him with my mouth gritted, "Jun Pyo, now isn't the time to focus on technicalities. I don't even want to know how you got her here, let alone understand that we are about to enter another country. Do you know how many laws you've broken? I mean, what have you made me an accessory to? I say with my mind leaping all over the place.

I know..I know I'm sorry, but I couldn't leave her with them... not again. If I just had more time to talk with her, I could make her come to her senses.

Well, according to this, I say, looking down at my watch. You've got an hour and a half before this train makes it to London. And you've got the same amount of time to explain to me how all of this" I say, pointing between him and his unconscious sister, "is going to help me free Violetta".

I've got it handled, he says. For the next 20 minutes, Jun Pyo releases footage directly to Violetta's legal team, sharing information about the Lotus organization—a copy of financial statements from the Lotus providing details that prove Violetta's innocence. And in releasing an anonymous video in which he confesses, he also said he'll be sending the information to Violetta's lawyer, Travis. At the mention of his name, my eyes glaze over, thinking about his promise when I get back, to see where things could go.

But looking at Jun Pyo, frantic and thinking about all the laws I've helped him break, and knowingly putting a target on my back. I know I've made my choice on who I want to take a risk on.

Once we've established the release time for the evidence supporting Violetta's acquittal, I notice some movement on the bed; it appears Suni is finally coming to, as she moans lightly. The platinum blonde hair from earlier is spread out on a pillowcase, and somehow she looks even taller with her neck elongated. But the quiet and confusion don't last for long as she sits up slowly at first, but her eyes shoot open fast as if she's remembering the events that led up to this moment.

I look over at Jun Pyo, but he seems frozen, almost impaled by her waking and sudden movement. I want to intervene, but this is his sister...his responsibility. I'm in enough trouble as it is, helping transport a woman into another country.

Jun Pyo, I say loudly, trying to wake him out of this stupor. His eyes look at me like he's forgotten I'm even in the room. But he recovers quickly, nodding his head.

Suni is now fully sitting up. I'm surprised she hasn't done anything wild, like try to get up and run, but instead she stares mainly at Jun Pyo and a little at me. I guess not seeing your sibling for over a decade will do that to you. As Jun Pyo explained it to me, the Lotus wouldn't even let Suni talk to him. They halted communication with them as they grew older. I can feel the tension in the small room, and I wish I could roll down the large window overlooking the rolling hills we pass by now, over halfway to London. Feeling a mix of uncertainty and awkwardness, I look at Jun Pyo and raise my eyebrows, tilting my head towards his sister.

"Talk now, we haven't got much time."

He nods his head in agreement with me and starts slowly.

"Suni, I don't know what to say. I am sorry I had to get you here in this way, but there was no other option. The Lotus has to go down for what they've done, and you're my sister. I couldn't just leave you there. I am willing to figure things out for us both if it means our freedom. The Lotus has taken enough from us already."

His brief but touching speech makes me want to shed a tear, but looking at Suni's face, she seems cold and unfazed. Her lips melt into a thin line, and her cheeks are hollow. For a few minutes, she stares, but then something unexpected happens. A laugh erupts from her, and the octaves she reaches tell me it's from her gut. My eyes are fixed on her as shock sets in. *Why is she laughing?*

"Listen, you are not my brother...he's been gone a long time, way before you decided to betray our family?

I look at Jun Pyo, and his eyes seem like a fire waiting to combust. He bites his lip hard but quickly recovers from his sister's words.

"Family...those people are not your family...they trafficked us into another country and forced us to be loyal to a criminal organization in exchange for food and shelter."

He says quickly, but it doesn't stop Suni.

You're right, but where else would we be, Jun…huh? With a traitor as a father and a mother who was an outcast in North Korea, what would you expect? The Lotus looked out for us when no one else would. They are the ones who ensured your papers looked legitimate to join the military. They are the ones who made sure I didn't turn into some street whore, and you didn't turn into a nobody with nothing to your name. They have given us life, and you betrayed them all for a woman, I hear. Everything they've done has been for us to survive, but that wasn't enough for you. You had to go and fall in love with some black bitc—

Suni, I am warning you now, don't finish that sentence. Disrespecting Maverick is like disrespecting me, and I won't tolerate it. Survival, eventually, you have to get out of survival mode, but I can see you're still stuck there. Suni think about it. Why would they keep us separated for so long if they wanted us to be family? Is it a coincidence that we've lived in the same city for ten years and you've never even been allowed to see me, talk to me, or visit? Suni, I am your only blood family, and yet they separate us and have us do terrible things. They have you serving as some madame while I'm doing their dirty work in the military. Is that really what a family would do to someone they love?

Jun Pyo throws his fingers in the air, making air quotations. I can tell he's not done, but he takes a breath, allowing his words to sink into the air of the cabin.

They told me you were off doing missions ... they never told me you were so close," Suni says. Her voice sounds like that of a child and is so low you can barely hear her over the sound of the train. She continues in the same low tone after a few moments. "They wouldn't lie to me about that...why would they do that? It seems like she's speaking more to herself rather than me or Jun Pyo.

Jun Pyo takes this opportunity to continue speaking the truth about the Lotus, going into detail about how they've controlled every aspect of their lives since childhood. Each piece of their lives revolved around the Lotus, forcing them onto a path they carved out for Jun Pyo to keep Suni submissive and in control of the women in the organization.

Staring in between them makes me feel like a fly on the wall, and looking at Suni's face after Jun Pyo provides a revelation of how dirty things are in the organization, Suni's face drops.

" I knew they were not the best people around, but I thought they were better than what you've described. The women I helped were real to me ...being able to teach them how to operate within the organization was all I did, we never did anything I would be ashamed of".

I stare at Suni, and it dawns on me that she's naive and blinded by what these people have done for her that she doesn't even realize what she's been a part of. An organization that traffics people and creates killers and political chameleons. There is no clear sign of why their paths were so different. Suni seems to have been shielded from the bad, and although she knew what was going on was illegal, I have to believe the little girl in her grew to accept it. That what she didn't know wouldn't hurt her, but it's left a door open for her to be manipulated.

Suni and Jun Pyo continue talking, and it seems their conversation is shifting from defensiveness to mutual disbelief. They talk about the different things multiple people fed them to keep them apart. The extensive control that dictates every single thing they've done. And one of the most heart-wrenching is the knowledge that it felt like there was no way out. My heart hurts thinking of a life that isn't your own..a life that can never just be.

I look at my watch again, checking the time... "We've got just under a half hour before we get to London..Jun, what's your plan?"

He stares at his sister with eyes more reserved and calm, then looks back at me, and the fire inside him comes to life as his eyes turn amber.

"We can't go back to Seoul, and Paris is too risky right now..I think it's best if we disappear once we get to London. I have some backdoor channels we can use to leave the country, but once we go, we'll never be able to come back. Are you both ready for that? He asks the question to us both, but is looking me squarely in the eyes as he says it.

" I don't think it would be wise to do this, but I'll be damned if I associate myself with those liars ever again. It's time I start living for myself," Suni says energetically, getting off the bed and slapping palms with Jun Pyo. Hyoeng, she says, which means brother in Korean.

I look between them both, feeling like an outsider. Jun Pyo doesn't wait for me to speak. He excuses himself and grabs my hand, leading me back to the connecting suite.

Maverick, we should talk about what I said in there... are you sure this is the life for you? A life on the run, never being able to see your family, all for...for me. He says, brazenly grabbing my hands and staring deep into my soul.

I pull away quickly and start pacing. "I ...I don't know, on one hand. I don't want to walk away from you again. I mean, what we have is like nothing I've ever felt before. But not being able to see my family. I don't know if I can do that. There's got to be another way. Maybe we can try to force the Lotus to expose themselves, and you'll be safe, I mean, INTERPOL would have to listen to you then. My words spill out of my mouth quickly like a dripping faucet filling up the tub, but even I know this isn't what's going to happen. For things to magically work themselves out, and no one ends up being collateral damage.

"Maverick, love it doesn't work like that, you know as well as I do they will kill me, you, and Suni. I understand what it means not to be close to family and lose the ones you care the most about. I don't want that for you. I want to be selfish because you deserve—no, you belong to be right here next to me.

I stare deep into his eyes and know the truth hurts. The truth is, I love him, and I know that if we could have one honest shot at a truthful life together, it would probably be the best thing that's ever happened to me. The love I'd been yearning for could be mine. But at what cost, the cost of all the other valuable relationships in my life? That's the cost.

I close my eyes as Jun Pyo holds me in his arms. I can see clear as day the people I love: my father, mother, and Shaunie. I see the Arthur J. Ravenel Bridge in Charleston and how its tall steel support beams shine under the street lights. I smell the sea salt in the air near the beach. All of what I'm familiar with would be gone in the blink of an eye. I feel paralyzed with indecision because I want to follow my heart, but my brain points out the logic that this decision doesn't make sense.

My choice, or lack of one, sinks deep into my chest, and tears start to stream down my face. ***We'll never see each other again, for real this time.***

I cry hard into Jun Pyo's arms and feel my shoulders shake and move up and down. I can't believe this is the end. It feels like my tears are endless, and as I overhear the train announcement that we'll be in London in fifteen minutes, I can't help but feel like I need to voice my decision and fast. The struggle to pull myself together and wipe away a few tears still falling seems like a task I can't complete, but I do.

"Jun," I say slowly, "It's not fair. Every time it seems like there's an us, it never can go anywhere because life keeps getting in the way." I don't know if choosing between love and family could ever be the right choice. And all of this I say, swinging my hands wildly, all of this you've done and sacrificed, and still neither of us can get what we want. But I can't just disappear from my loved ones. I wish I could choose you, but I just can't.

He grabs my chin and anchors me into him. "I know this isn't what either of us wanted, but I'd rather you be living a life in the light than one in the shadows with me. What kind of man would I be to subject you to that? I wouldn't dream it. For now, it's not safe for us ...but maybe we could meet again later in life. His eyes seem to shift away from me at the mention of his last sentence.

I know this isn't what either of us thought, but maybe this is what our time with one another was supposed to be. Two ships passing by and being in front of the other briefly, just moments. And even if it was just a moment, I'm going to remember you... Maverick Robinson. I'll remember you forever. The kiss we share is so deep, sweeping me in like waves from the ocean, pulling me under. His lips caress mine, and he doesn't let go. It almost feels like we could suffocate one another, but there's no letting go.

A light knock on the connecting door stirs us both, but it's just Suni. She averts her eyes from us, appearing to have interrupted our one last private moment. Her face reads apologetic, but she steps further into the cabin.

We're almost there; we need to move. I'm sure the Lotus has tracked me. Jun ...are you ready?

He looks at me, lost in his thoughts, and shakes his head. Yes, almost, but before we disappear, I need to get Maverick to safety, back to the States.

I should be fine...I'm not wanted for anything besides I've answered all of the authorities' questions; they do not need to stop me from going home".

It's not them I'm worried about; the Lotus has many connections with traffickers and border patrol in different countries. Just let me help you...it'll be the last thing I do." Squeezing my hand for reassurance, I try to match his smile, but it doesn't match up.

"Okay, get me home," I say.

Suni, I need a moment alone with Maverick. Please leave us.

Alright, but hurry up, we'll have to be on the move as soon as we stop in London. She exits and notices Jun Pyo fumbling with something in his pockets.

"I never got the chance to give you this," he pulls out a black velvet jewelry box and opens it up, facing me—a ring: a princess-cut diamond in the center, with light blue gemstones around it.

What is this? What is this for?

It would have been your engagement ring. I know you loved the color blue... and I don't know if things could have worked out that way. But I want you to keep it.. you must have something to remember me by.

My nerves are all over the place again, the roller coaster in me just climbed 3000 feet and is about to drop into oblivion. An engagement ring?

Wow is all I can say for a few minutes as I try my best to become coherent.

I know it wasn't what you were expecting, right? I'm sorry I didn't have time to figure out your ring size or know what type of jewelry you like, I just——

Jun Pyo, don't apologize, it's perfect...can you put it on me? I want to see how it feels.

He stops stammering and smiles at me, the smile that he's tried to hide from the world. But he's not hiding, not right now.

The ring is a little loose on my finger and naturally looks out of place to me since I don't wear rings. But looking at my left hand, the beauty of what the ring means fills my heart in a way I can't fully describe.

This is perfect," I say, kissing him as if my life depended on it.

V

Part Five

Chapter 18: Meant To Be

10 Years Later

"Happy birthday, from an old friend."

The postcard has no return address and features a photo of Java, Indonesia, an island located in the middle of the Pacific Ocean. I stare at the card, knowing who the sender is. Even after all these years, we both still hold a place in each other's hearts. It appears that on the eve of my fortieth birthday, this postcard landed on my doorstep. There's only one person who sends me postcards. I relish the card and think, "Was it ever meant to be?"

Luckily for me, no one else was home. Travis is at a meeting with the judges in the Sixth District, and Jade, our daughter, is at a playmate with a friend from school.

I turn the postcard over several times in my hand and push my head back against the comfy sofa recliner. I think of the whirlwind of emotions I felt almost ten years ago, the love, agony, and defeat of truly not being able to live out my fantasy with him. I imagine a life full of love, yet one where I would always have to look over my shoulder for threats. I love my life, but I'd be damned if I didn't think of the what-ifs that plague my mind when it comes to him.

It's been over a decade since I have even spoken that man's name. I am not as young as I used to be. Life looks different at forty. There are no fancy trips or jobs abroad. Covert missions and espionage are far behind me, as I've settled into a more normal-looking life as a government employee by day and a mother and wife by night.

When I returned to the States, I would have thought a welcome party from INTERPOL would be waiting for me.

The trail of mess left in Paris created a wake of confusion. The Lotus organization wanted Jun Pyo's head. I'm sure he told some of their secrets and exposed them all for the sake of family and to right a wrong against me. I'll never forget the lengths he went to do the right thing. He blew up his life for me, and it's the most sincere thing any man has ever done for me. But that type of love doesn't sustain itself when life or death choices exist in every moment. No one will ever make my heart skip a beat and turn my insides into a fire that destroys everything in its path.

But there is someone who came close. He just didn't get to me first.

I became Mrs. Travis Spencer about eight years ago after a year of serious dating. We had an intimate beach wedding ceremony in my hometown. The ceremony was immediate family only and one of the best days of my life. It felt like something out of a fairy tale. After years of heartbreak and unfulfilled chances at love, I believed I had finally found the one. It wasn't long after getting married that I became pregnant with Jade, our miracle baby.

Jade Miracle Spencer was named after her grandmother, Travis's mom, who passed away from cancer when he was sixteen. She's got the best of us, with her wide doe eyes like mine and a smile like Travis's. Although she's only eight, she has the personality of a thirty-year-old because she's always hanging around her parents. My baby is the greatest thing I've ever had a part in creating. I used to wonder whether she looked and acted like the kind of person my first child could've been. She truly was what I needed over the last few years of my life.

After years of believing I could never conceive again, and thinking God had a sick sense of humor because I had aborted my first baby, I felt like I could finally breathe once I found out I was pregnant. I remember praying harder than I ever had that I would have a healthy pregnancy and that my "little bean" would sprout. The pregnancy consisted of becoming diabetic, losing bits of my hair, and being put on bed rest around my seventh month. The doctors were so nervous that, due to my health conditions, I wouldn't be able to carry to term. But my husband, Travis, was never nervous. He was with me at every appointment and took care of me like a champ through my irritable mood swings and overly emotional hormones that sometimes made him come home in the middle of the day.

But somewhere along the line, things had changed in our marriage; the man who brought a new spark to my life started to dim. It wasn't just his fault. This was a joint effort. Our baby Jade, who wasn't a baby anymore, was now almost eight years old. My time as a stay-at-home mom, along with notes on my military record, left my permanent file so derailed that I was unable to do much in my career. I spent many years taking care of my family, the thing I had wanted for so long, but running a family was much more complicated than I thought. It was a thankless job most days, balancing a child and my husband's ambitions and goals. The years had turned me into some weird trophy wife who showed up to important dinners that validated my husband's character. There was no room for Maverick Robinson anymore, only Maverick Spencer.

My military skills seemed to disappear, and until recently, I was bored out of my mind as a family woman. My recent jump back into drone intelligence with the government is thanks to an old friend, Drea. She was able to pull some strings and get me a position. With my skills, the job is a breeze, but new technology makes it almost impossible not to feel like you're constantly under surveillance.

Being fortunate enough to watch my daughter grow up has been the greatest reward, and thanks to Travis's excellent ability to provide for us, I have been able to put off working.

His small law firm in the shopping strip in Richmond, VA, had long transformed into an impressive firm that represented some of the most prominent political figures in the D.C. area. After Violetta's acquittal, based on the evidence Jun Pyo provided, people were beating down Travis's door for representation. He became the overnight lawyer everyone wanted as their legal counsel. His office turned into an executive suite on the fifteenth floor of a D.C. high-rise building in the business district. For a few years, that was enough for my husband. But then his business associate, who also happened to be a lawyer, her name was Farrah Clove, suggested his path to the judicial bench would be a much better use of his time.

Farrah Clove was a gorgeous white woman with strawberry blonde hair, a curvy figure, and a butt like a Black girl's. She went from being my husband's most prominent supporter to becoming a judge and serving as his second in command. I couldn't stand her and suspected that if she hadn't already slept with my husband, she had it on her to-do list. A Harvard-educated summa cum laude graduate, she had been raised in a wealthy family in Massachusetts and worked on a few cases with Travis. He was so impressed by the courtroom performance that he hired her and never looked back. Over many cocktail parties and social outings with Travis, I'd learned all these things.

Her accomplishments compared to mine didn't bother me, but it was the way she would place her hands on the small of Travis's back, even when I was standing in front of him. The way she intimately touched him disturbed me.

The truth was, my marriage was good, but times had been hard and had changed us both. The string that held us together, I wish it were love or God, as it should have been, but really, it was our love for Jade and my husband's fear of the public scrutiny he would face as one of the two Black male judges in his district. The unimaginable pressure he faced took a brutal hit on our marriage.

The man I met in Richmond was utterly different from the man I know today. The Travis I used to know was attentive to me, caring, and humorous. He could make me laugh and show our relationship effort in ways that made me fall back in love with him. But now—now he was more focused on being a judge than a father and husband. Instead of being a pillar of emotional strength, I found his desire to be a powerful man to be the only area where he showed room for emotion these days.

But again, it wasn't his entire fault; I had changed, too. About three years into our marriage, Shaunie had been the victim of a nasty domestic violence dispute. She was still seeing a married man and thought her fairy tale was finally being orchestrated. He had finally left his wife for Shaunie, and she was living the life, with her own salon and fancy clients, until one night, when the wife showed up at her shop pretending to have a consultation. She pulled out a weapon and killed Shaunie.

After finding out about the affair and just how long it had been going on, the wife was livid. It didn't take long to find her, but Shaunie was gone. My best friend, the person I could tell everything to, was gone in an instant. My heart hardened after that, and not much room was left for intimacy. My parents didn't know how to handle the news, and my mother had a nervous breakdown. All I felt for a while was rage. Not even Jade's face could simmer down the hurt I felt. Shaunie, she was the one I could always trust to keep my secrets.

But my marriage recovered once I finally forgave Shaunie for even putting herself in that type of predicament, and I forgave her boyfriend's wife as well. I was able to let my husband in again after taking a couple of months of therapy.

Somehow, as he transitioned from law practice to the bench, our love for one another grew again. We had reignited a fire that seemed to have dulled. We were reconnecting in a way I hadn't seen in years, but it didn't last, because life continued happening. After trying to get pregnant for a second time, which resulted in two miscarriages over the course of three years, the emotional toll it took on me was overwhelming. Even a season in therapy couldn't fix this, and so our marriage crumbled again. Travis became consumed with work, and I became consumed with caring for Jade and grieving my sister's death.

I live in a 3,000-square-foot house in a sophisticated neighborhood with manicured lawns. My daughter attends private school, and all of my financial needs are met. Between my husband's income and a monthly retirement check from the Force, I have no monetary concerns. However, at forty years old, on my birthday, this is not how I thought my life with Travis would look. We are supposed to be focused on walking with each other until the end, but lately, we've just been managing, not really living.

Which brings me back to the postcard I hold in my hands? I feel like a giddy schoolgirl, knowing who the sender is. I can't help but smell it, thinking there might be some fragrance that reminds me of how he used to smell. I'm not sure how to feel about the fact that he knows where I live, even after all this time; his ability to find me and watch me is strange, yet protective.

Opening my jewelry box, I reach for the Tiffany bracelet and chain Travis got for our fifth anniversary. Next to it is the ring from all those years ago, the diamond and blue gemstones still shining in the light. I touch it and put it on my finger, remembering the feeling of the first time I wore it. I admire my hand, taking off my simple gold wedding band for a moment, but quickly put the ring back in its spot in my jewelry box.

As time passes and draws closer to evening, I take a shower, preparing for my birthday dinner with Travis. It has become a tradition for us to have a great meal at Chatsworth's, an upscale Italian restaurant, and take a horse-drawn carriage ride through the uptown area. This year, since Jade finally has a friend whose parents I trust for sleepovers, it will be just the two of us.

I refresh myself and put on a red, sparkly gown that ends right above my knees. The manicure and pedicure from earlier in the week make my hands and feet pop with cherry red nail polish. I put a little makeup around my eyes, which now have a few wrinkles at the edges, and add a few embellishments to my natural hair, which falls well past my shoulders. A few stray gray strands I tuck behind my ear.

With soft shades of gold, smoky eye shadow, and a layer of

brown matte lipstick, I feel ready for Travis's arrival at any moment. I walk downstairs into our den, with its decked-out bar and large flat-screen TV, and grab a bottle of whiskey without a glass. I take a quick shot, steadying myself for the night.

I slip off my uncomfortable but expensive heels and sit in the recliner where my husband usually sits on Sunday evenings during football season. I close my eyes, thinking, this is what four decades look like, smirking and feeling full of pride.

***

My phone blares the alarm I set to prepare for our eight o'clock reservation.

I check the time. It's seven p.m. I get up from the recliner and walk to the window facing our front yard and three-car garage. I don't see Travis's car in the driveway, and I find it strange. He should have been back at least two hours ago from his meeting.

I call his phone, and it goes straight to voicemail. I stare at the screen, unsettled. He always answers my calls. I try again and let it ring a few times. This time, he answers immediately.

With my ear pressed close to the phone, I ask, "Travis, where are you? I can't hear you. It's almost time for our reservation."

Instead of a response, all I hear is background noise, loud cars passing by, and horns blaring. I pull the phone away from my ear, confused, when a notification flashes across the screen.

"Travis appears to have been in a car accident. Would you like to call 911 and share his location?"

Our phones are connected and set to trigger alerts if the system detects something serious. I don't hesitate. I tap "Yes."

I check the location. He's on the other side of town, nowhere near his office.

I rush upstairs, quickly changing into regular clothes, then hurry to my car. My hands tremble as I start the engine and drive as fast as I safely can, praying under my breath as I race toward his location.

Chapter 19 Bonus: Goodbye For Now

Present Day

It's been exactly three weeks since I found out about my husband's affair of all days on my fortieth birthday.

I pulled up to Midtown, a contemporary part of the city known for young twenty-somethings, feeling completely out of place in a pair of old sneakers and workout clothes. I saw my husband's BMW 7 Series smashed into the front bumper of a gray Nissan Altima. I exited my car, ready to make sure he was okay, when I noticed him sitting in an ambulance near the accident scene.

The front end of his vehicle was scratched beyond recognition, the midnight blue paint chipped, and shattered glass scattered across the ground. I picked up my pace, walking faster toward the ambulance, when a woman came into view, rubbing Travis's shoulder and arm, which were in a sling.

They didn't notice me, and I debated turning on my heels and going back to my car, pretending I hadn't seen anything. But then I remembered it was my birthday, and my husband was acting like a fool in public.

I walked up, ready to catch them by surprise, when I was stopped by the police officer assisting with the accident.

"Excuse me, miss, you can't come through here. There's

been an accident."

"Oh, I know. That's actually my husband right over there," I said, pointing to the ambulance. The officer steps aside, looking stunned.

I was finally within eyesight, and Travis noticed me first, the smile quickly fading from his face. None other than Farrah is standing by his side. She looks even more surprised by my presence and tries to create an appropriate distance between her and Travis. But it was too late. It didn't take a law degree to know something inappropriate was going on.

"Hey, baby, I was just about to call you. Farrah and me..." He paused. "You remember her, my colleague," he said, trying to refresh my memory and signal that she worked with him.

How could I forget?

"Mrs. Spencer, pleased to see you again," I say, falsely extending my hand to shake hers.

I glare a hole through Travis and asked him to step to the side of the ambulance so we could talk in private. The old Maverick was dying to make an appearance, but the last time I lost my temper over a man and decided to beat someone's ass was a long time ago in a bowling alley.

Mrs. Spencer has a different strategy, I reminded myself.

The days since the accident had made it painfully obvious that my husband no longer cared about our marriage. He had stayed home at least five times in three weeks, mostly to make things look normal for Jade. But as soon as she lay down for the night, he would leave. I didn't bother asking where he was headed, because I already knew the answer.

Although he was apologetic and swore nothing was going on, I knew better. The thought of him with another woman repulsed me, yet I couldn't help feeling like a hypocrite as I thought about my own feelings for another man.

We hadn't spoken since his car accident on my birthday, when I discovered he was having an affair. I politely instructed him to grab his things before he found them on our gas range grill, being chargrilled. We tried to remain cordial and figure out how to tell Jade that we would be separating, but we hadn't had the heart to even start that conversation.

"Mommy, it's the phone. It's for you."

I looked up at Jade, puzzled that her emergency cell phone was ringing. No one even had this number. Maybe it was Travis, I thought.

I had blocked his number on my phone, and we only spoke occasionally when he came by to pick Jade up. Part of me wanted to believe it was him on the line, begging for my forgiveness.

I looked down at the screen and saw that the number was international, though I couldn't tell from where. A strange, gnawing feeling passed over me, and I debated whether I should even answer. This wasn't Travis calling.

"Hello, who is calling this number?" I ask cautiously.

"This is Suni... I need your help. It's about Jun Pyo."

I stare down at the phone and can't believe my ears. Ten years. Ten years, and they call my daughter's phone. The same throaty voice I remember hearing only for a short while from that train ride to London rings in my ears. Suni sounds older, but still the same.

I look at Jade, who has gone back to playing her zombie video game and has no clue what's going on. Glancing between the phone and Jade, I leave the upstairs loft and walk directly into the master bedroom.

"Suni... this is unexpected. I want to ask how you even got this number, but I know Jun Pyo always had his strange ways of getting things done, so I guess you're no different. Why are you calling me, and what would you possibly think I can do?" I speak pointedly and try not to let my emotions show.

"Maverick, believe me, I know my brother promised never to reach back out for safety reasons, and he doesn't know I'm calling you, but there is no one else. I know you don't deserve this; you deserve to be left alone. But Jun Pyo needs you..." "He needs you," she says, her voice breaking.

My heart hears the way she says need, and I can't help but feel the thump in my chest as the blood begins to simmer with uncertainty. Steadying my hands on the column of my bed, I try to be persistent and get more specifics.

"Suni, that's not really enough to go off of... I mean, it's been ten years. I'm not entirely sure you called me because I'm the person who could help your brother. He's... he's a ghost, and you are supposed to be too."

"Look, I can't explain over the phone, but all I can tell you is he needs"

"I understand, but that's not good enough. I'm not just hopping on a plane because you called me. I have a life of my own, a family... and long gone are the days of me just jumping when someone says, 'How high?' I'm sorry, but I can't help you."

"Maverick, he's... he's going to die. It's" She hesitates. "I think it's a broken heart. He needs to see you."

My heart sinks, and so do I, sliding to the floor. Die? It's too soon. He's not that old. This can't be true. "What do you mean, a broken heart that's not real, Suni. And whatever joke you're playing right now, it's cruel.

"Maverick... are you hearing me? I said"

"Suni."

"I heard what you said, and it doesn't change my answer. Is this some sick joke to have you call me and pretend he's hurt just to see if I'll come running? It isn't right, Suni. Get off my daughter's phone and don't ever call this number again. This isn't just goodbye for now, it's forever." I say, and then I disconnect the call.

My pulse pounds, and my head feels inflamed, like the room temperature has climbed to one hundred degrees. I can't believe I just said that, but my words only reflect half the truth. I am intrigued, awakened by the curiosity of seeing Jun Pyo again, but also terrified of what I might find if he truly is dying.

I wonder what he's like now, whether the gray hairs so prominent on my own head mirror his. I wonder if he ever found someone else or started a family of his own. For him, the ultimate joy in life would have been family. Most of all, I wonder if he still feels the same if the man who gave me an engagement ring on a train in London still carries a torch for me.

But I am not some young, love-struck girl anymore. I'm a woman, and I have Jade to think about. Traveling across the world and chasing after him is no longer who I am. That chapter closed long ago, leaving a mess in its wake. He's my past, and Jade is my present, my future, and everything in between.

I hear Jade at the door, peeking in, unsure of how much she's heard. I turn my back to her for a moment, wiping away a few hot, angry, stray tears.

"Mommy, are you good?" Jade asks, her sweet voice softening my anger.

"Mommy's just fine, baby. I just had to say goodbye to an old friend, that's all. I'm alright, promise," I say.

"I don't believe you," she says, sticking her thumb out.

Walking toward the doorway, I wrap my arms around her shoulders in a bear hug.

"Baby, I promise." I extend my pinky to hers, linking them together.

THE END

For now